Shoot-out at San Lorenzo

Blue gunsmoke rolls as a vicious gang of killers puts the homes of Arizona settlers to the flames. Who is behind the terror attacks?

Security man James Slaughter suspects the mayor of San Lorenzo, Joe Hagerty, may be the mastermind for he is buying up the settlers' dispossessed land cheap and fast. Does the mayor's haughtily beautiful wife, Jane, know more than she reveals? And who is the mysterious Mr Black who arrives at their casino in a private stagecoach in the middle of the night?

Now the trouble comes thick and fast as Slaughter searches for the gang's hideout and their psychopathic leader. Lightning strikes and guns thunder!

Shoot-out at San Lorenzo

HENRY REMINGTON

A Black Horse Western

ROBERT HALE · LONDON

Typeset by
Derek Doyle & Associates, Shaw Heath
Printed and bound in Great Britain by
CPI Antony Rowe, Chippenham and Eastbourne

ONE

The locomotive's warning bell clanged mournfully as it threaded its way through the desolate gorges of southern Arizona. The grimy-faced engineer peered ahead through his goggles as they ate up the narrow track and shouted to his stoker, 'Keep piling them logs in the furnace, Jed. We don't wanna lose pressure.'

Clouds of black smoke rasped from the engine's tall stack as the sturdy iron horse hauled steel girders and heavy mining equipment on two flatbed trucks, a barred and locked caboose and a passenger coach up an incline.

'Ah'm feedin' her fast as I can,' the negro, Jed, whined, sweat dripping from his half-naked body.

Six guards, in Western garb, carbines at the ready, sat in various positions on the girders and about the caboose as the train went rocking on its way. They did not notice a man in a buckskin shirt haul himself up from the observation platform at the rear of the coach and clamber along its roof, his left hand hanging on to the brim of his leather hat, his right steadying the heavy revolver slung on his hip. His slits of eyes narrowed against the grit and smoke, he leaped on to the roof of the armoured caboose and, with feline lightness lowered himself down to land beside one of the guards.

'Howdy, Mason,' he yelled. 'Any sign of trouble?'

'Ain't no sign of nuthin',' the man rasped out. 'No 'Paches, no Mex'cuns, nobody. I figure we been sold false information.'

'Good,' James Slaughter muttered. 'We're making good time. Should be at San Lorenzo in an hour or so. About thirty more miles to go.'

He waited awhile then shouted, 'I'll be gittin' back to the coach.'

'Yeah? Given yaself the easy job?' Mason jeered. 'Riding in comfort.'

A grin creased Slaughter's dark, rutted face. 'Aw, they may have planted somebody *inside*. You jest keep your eyes peeled, pal.'

He climbed lithely back on to the roof of the caboose and made his way along to drop down on to the platform, pushing into the coach. There was a mixed bunch of passengers, miners, storekeepers with, among them two rough-looking *hombres* he didn't much like the look of. There was one smartly attired young woman, sitting by a window with her

6

back to the engine.

Slaughter lowered himself on to the hard-slatted seat opposite her but on the aisle side so he could keep an eye on the *hombres*. Comely females of the respectable sort were few and far between on the frontier and he studied her through his narrowed lids as the ties of the single track clicked rhythmically beneath them and smoke clouds billowed past.

The young lady in question was attired in a dove-grey travelling costume, a blue chiffon scarf wound around her throat, which highlighted the pale blue of her eyes. Thick braids of corn-coloured hair were wound back beneath a wide-brimmed grey felt hat, decorated again with a bandanna of blue. 'Very nice,' Slaughter muttered, as he watched her heavy bosom beneath her tight-waisted jacket swaying to the motion of the train.

Jane Hagerty pretended not to notice the broad-chested prairie rat who had settled himself down and stared at her so insolently as the carriage clattered along. He had tossed his hat down on to the empty seat opposite her and his thick black hair fell across a face as deeply tanned as saddle leather. Around his forehead was a crimson headband, not unlike that an Apache might wear. Indeed, his dark muscular diaphragm, revealed by his open buckskin shirt, indicated he might have Indian blood. Typical half-Indian trash of the frontier, she thought.

7

Mrs Hagerty entwined her fingers across her lap so that the mongrel would get a good view of her gold wedding ring. She gave a snort of disgust when he had the temerity to raise his legs, encased in bleached and torn blue jeans, and rested his filthy boots on the vacant seat beside her. She jerked her skirt away, glanced out of the window at the dreary landscape flitting by, and closed her eyes in a pretence of sleep.

' 'Scuse me, ma'am,' Slaughter drawled, his green eyes gleaming with mischief as he regarded her. 'You don't mind if I make myself comfortable.'

Jane Hagerty ignored him, but after a while she could not resist glancing at him through her lashes. Through the holes in his jeans were displayed faded pink long johns and, as if guessing he was being watched, the ruffian reached a hand down and eased a tightness about his crotch.

'You know somethang?' he suddenly drawled. 'You're a damn fine-looking lady.'

Jane eyed him with disapproval, touched her nose with a dainty finger and fanned herself with a magazine, continuing to ignore him.

'Yeah, waal,' he said, 'I guess you knew that already. What takes you to San Lorenzo?'

'This train takes me,' she replied, severely. 'To meet my husband.'

'An' who might he be?'

'You've not heard of Joe Hagerty, Mayor of San

8

Lorenzo del Rio and land agent?' she queried with some pride.

'Oh, *him*. Land-*grabber* might be a more accurate description.'

'What?' The lady's tone rose shrill. 'Just who do you think—?'

'Aw, don't let the lootenant git ya riled up, ma'am.' Whatever she was going to say was cut short by a wiry little man who came swaying along the aisle, a rifle clutched to his chest. He clambered over Slaughter's legs, sat down opposite her and emitted a caustic cackle. 'He's only needlin' ya for a bit of fun.'

'Lieutenant?' Her words were incredulous. 'All the officers of our army I've met have been gentlemen. They look and behave like it. They don't sprawl with their boots up on seats in public.'

'Us Confederates is more easy-going, ma'am.' A smile twitched Aaron Snipe's pointy-nosed, under-nourished features. 'The lootenant cain't help himself. It's like a red rag to a bull, him seein'a fine-trottin' lady like you.'

'War's over long time ago, Aaron,' Slaughter drawled sleepily, hoicking his gunbelt around his waist so the heavy Schofield six-gun hung across his loins. 'I ain't a lootenant any more.'

'I see,' Jane Hagerty commented, primly. 'A former Confederate. That explains the oafish behaviour. You can't bear to admit that you lost.'

9

She recoiled sharply as Slaughter sprang to his feet and leaned across her, as if fearing he might hit her. But he was peering out of the window. He had seen the flash of light on steel up on the hillside. It had to be a knife or gun. 'Christ Awmighty!' he shouted. 'We're under attack.'

'Where?' Aaron asked.

'Up there. Use your eyes, man. I can see one, two, three of them.' He knelt to hoist out his Spencer carbine from under the seat, levered the trigger guard and fed a .52 from the tubular magazine into the breech. 'Excuse me, ma'am.' He leaned across her knees, poked the barrel through the open window and took aim, thumbing back the firing hammer. Jane Hagerty stared at him, speechless. 'Keep well back,' he advised her.

But at that moment the train seemed to shudder on its track and from up front came the huge roar of an explosion. All in the compartment hung tight to their seats as the carriage began creaking, swaying and almost frog-hopping along the rails. Up ahead the engine was knocked off the track as the hidden barrels of gunpowder blew up with the force of a cannon. As it tipped to its side the flatbeds piled with steel girders were skewed into the air, followed by the armoured caboose and the men guarding it. Back inside the carriage there was a grating and squealing of torn wood and metal and, as if in slow motion, as men hung desperately to

10

their seats, they were pitched sideways. There was chaos as the passengers were tumbled about and the whole train slid to a halt on its side.

As the dust cleared, Slaughter found himself lying on top of Jane Hagerty, with Snipe sprawled on top of him. Her hat had been dislodged and her hair was over her eyes as Slaughter's chest was pressed tight upon her bosom. 'Hell's bells,' he muttered. 'Never thought we'd git close acquainted so soon.'

'Get off me, you pig,' she screamed.

'I cain't. Aaron's got his damn boot on my head.'

Snipe was struggling to right himself amid the moans and confusion inside the lopsided compartment.

'Aaron, you heard what she said.' Slaughter couldn't help grinning at the look of fury in her blue eyes. 'Git yourself off of us. Are you all right, sweetheart?'

'What do you think?' she gasped.

The ex-lieutenant managed to get to his feet and pulled her upright, too. The window he had been peering from was now ten feet above them. He searched amid the mangled remains and found his Spencer. 'C'mon, Aaron. You go first. I'll give ya a leg up. Stand on my shoulders.'

There were shouts, screams and shots from outside as the little Snipe climbed up on him. 'I said my shoulders, dot my dose. Where's my damn hat

11

gawn?' He found it, crammed it on and tossed Aaron's rifle to him. 'I'll come up next.'

'What about me?' Jane wailed.

'You're safer staying here.'

'No,' she begged. 'You can't leave me.'

'OK. Can you climb up on the seat? Go on. I'll hold ya steady.' As she wobbled back and forth Slaughter was confronted by her shapely posterior encased in a voluminous skirt and petticoat. He tried to push her upwards with his spread palms and had a glimpse of black stockings. 'Oops! Sorry, ma'am,' he said, as his fingers slid up between her fleshy thighs. 'My hands slipped!'

'Let me go, you fool,' she screamed, as she grabbed hold of Aaron's wrist and he hauled her up through the open window.

'No need to kick. I was only tryin' to help.'

Slaughter passed his carbine to Aaron and climbed athletically up the slatted seats, leaping to pull himself into the open air. 'Jesus!' he whistled, as bullets panged off the side of the coach and a bunch of white-clothed Mexicans fired at them from the side of the hill. 'How many of them *are* there.'

It was like a duck-shoot. The guards and passengers who had survived the crash were being potted mercilessly by thirty or so attacking Mexicans. Slaughter knelt in front of the terrified woman, grabbed his Spencer and prepared to fight

12

alongside Snipe, exposed as they were on top of the side of the coach.

'It's gonna be a massacre,' Snipe opined. 'We ain't got a snowball's chance in hell.'

Aaron's long-barrelled Ben Henry buffalo gun, magnificent on the open plains, was unsuited for so close an encounter as this. It was almost impossible to get a bead on the enemy, who had started bounding down the hillside, dodging from rock to rock.

Slaughter squeezed out several fast shots with the Spencer and had the satisfaction in seeing one of the opposition go tumbling like an unlucky rabbit to lay still. 'Got him!' he gritted out, and fed another slug into the seven-shot to send another attacker pirouetting into eternity.

He was pleased to see that the two *hombres* who had aroused his suspicions had climbed from the train and were blamming away with revolvers in a fight for their own lives. He glanced along at the overturned flatbeds, the girders and boxes of cargo thrown on to the trackside.

The locomotive itself was derailed, half on its back, its wheels still churning, steaming and hissing like some wounded beast.

'That's three or four of the varmints accounted for, but there's still about twenty to go,' Aaron crowed, as he finally sent a Mexican to his maker.

'And more,' Slaughter groaned, as he spotted a

13

rider, clad in a billowing white cloak over his head and shoulders, like some Tuareg, charging along the track, followed by three other horsemen.

Seeing them come, the engineer and his stoker set off running back towards them, their oily faces panicked. Hit in the back by one of the horsemen's bullets, Jed stumbled on to his face and would not move again. Ever.

The leading horseman, in his white cloak, wielded a machete in his fist and swung it expertly as he caught up with the engineer. The man's head was severed, rolling along the track in a catherine wheel of blood.

The last of the guards, including Mason, who had jumped clear of the toppled caboose, were gunned down by the other horsemen, who hauled in, apparently aware of the valuable contents of the armoured van.

Aaron relevered his 15-shot, took careful aim and dislodged one from his saddle, the mustang bounding away free.

The murderous leader of the pack had gone galloping along past the train, swinging his machete at anyone in his way. Meanwhile his foot soldiers, yelling and shouting, were clambering over the train, shooting through the windows at anyone still alive inside.

'They're friggin' fanatics,' Aaron screamed. 'They mean to kill us all.'

This notion was reinforced by the fact that both of the *hombres*, one after the other, had caught lead and crumpled, falling one upon the other on to the track in a tangle of limbs.

Slaughter slung the empty Spencer by its strap over his shoulders, catching a look at Jane Hagerty's agonized face as she crouched low. He pulled out his nine-inch barrelled revolver and fought back as the bandits focused on them and bullets whined about them like angry bees.

'Aaron,' he shouted, 'try to grab that hoss that's roamin' free. We gotta git outa here.'

As Snipe slid from the side of the carriage bent double, Henry, rifle in hand, made a beeline to catch the nag. Slaughter saw the Arabian-clad *jefe* charging back towards them, machete held aloft. He took aim with the Schofield, but there was only the dull click of the hammer. His bullets were gone.

The *jefe* was coming full gallop, slicing his machete at anyone who presented himself. But not for long. Slaughter hurled himself. Rider and mount went crashing into the dust. The masked rider tried to slash at him with his machete, but Slaughter held him down. For moments, as they struggled, their eyes met, and his foe's were cold vivid blue ones, intense and fixed, a murderer's eyes. Slaughter slammed the heavy Schofield against his jaw and his opponent collapsed, out cold.

Slaughter had no time to finish him for there was a howl of anger as the bandits saw their chief in dire danger and ran along the track to help out.

The former lieutenant sprang up, holstered his revolver and caught hold of the dazed mustang which was gamely getting to its feet. With the agility of his part-Comanche ancestry, he swung into the saddle and hauled the horse around. 'Yee-hagh!' he yelled, the delirium of combat coursing through his veins, urging the mustang away.

'Jump!' he shouted, as he saw Jane Hagerty hesitating on the train. 'Or are you gonna stay there and git raped?'

The young woman visibly swallowed her fear and leapt, scrambling to hang on to the back of the mustang behind the saddle, her nails tearing into Slaughter's shirt for support. 'Hang on,' he shouted. 'Grab me round the waist. Don't be shy.'

Aaron had caught the stray, stuffed his rifle in the saddle boot and was firing his revolver in a rearguard action to keep the *bandidos* at bay.

'*Vayamos!*' his friend shouted, leading them in an arc around the back of the derailed train and heading away across the chaparral. 'Let's go, *muchachos!*'

TWO

Big Bucks Clayton, the owner of Copperolis Mine, was incandescent with fury. 'You mean you abandoned your men, rode out of there to save your own miserable skins?' he roared, slamming his fist on his office desk.

'To save hers, too.' Slaughter nodded at Jane Hagerty. 'There weren't much we could do about the rest, they were mostly gone.'

Clayton was a beefy man, his biceps bulging in a tight city suit, tugging at the bow tie tight around his collar, looking like he was about to have apoplexy. 'You just let them damn Mex'cuns help 'emselves to my payroll. Didn't you put up any fight?'

'You take them words back, mister.' Aaron Snipe squared up to him like an agressive bantam cock. 'We fought like the devils of Hell were after us. Look at this.' He pointed to a bullet crease across his cheek. 'We were lucky to get outa there alive.'

'OK, simmer down, both of you,' Slaughter drawled. 'If you're int'rested, in my opinion they weren't Mexicans to start with. You ever heard of *peons* in white pyjamas being crack shots?' They just put on them cotton clothes and *sombreros* to try to fool us. *Bandidos* would be wearing leathers. Mexicans are excitable, they shoot wild. Those boys were good shots.'

'Oh, yeah?' Bucks Clayton scowled. 'So what does that prove? Does that bring back my cash?'

'That guy in the cloak, *he* wasn't Mexican,' Slaughter mused. 'How many Mex'cuns you seen with icy blue eyes?'

Clayton's bluster had begun to cool. In his youth he had been a bare-knuckle prize-fighter and had a squashed nose to prove it. Now he was bald, big-gutted and middle-aged and was a renowned big spender, which accounted for his moniker, Big Bucks.

'If they weren't Mexes, who the hell were they?' he demanded. 'I paid you to guard that consignment. You said you could get it through.'

'You paid three hundred and another three hundred promised. How about settling up? We put our lives on the line. There's six of my men dead.'

'So you won't need to pay them, will you? You won't get another cent outa me, you panhandling bum. You've practically bankrupted me. You any idea how much that engine and track cost me? What am I gonna do, have another sent out all the way from England around Cape Horn? I oughta sue you.'

'You better watch your mouth, Mr Clayton,' Aaron cried, waggling his finger in his face. 'We don't take them words from any man.'

'Aw, forget it,' Slaughter said, sitting on the edge of the desk and helping himself to one of Big Bucks' cigars from a humidor. He struck a match on his heel and lit up. 'Buck's het up. Cain't blame him. Who *were* those jokers? Maybe we oughta try to find out. Maybe we owe that to Mr Clayton, Aaron. And to them who are dead. At least we can try.'

Jane Hagerty had been sitting on a chair silently, sipping at a mug of coffee. Suddenly she exploded. 'My God, there's been a massacre and all you do is squabble about whose fault it was, how much cash has been lost.'

James Slaughter regarded her curiously, recalling how she had hugged him tight around the waist as they rode, her breasts bobbing against his back with the movement of the horse. It had been a pleasant way to make their escape.

'You're upset, Mrs Hagerty,' Clayton soothed. 'You've been through a terrible ordeal. We'll get you back to your husband 'fore sundown, don't you worry. Only we've got a lot to think about here. Mr Hagerty's probably told you that out on the frontier money sometimes matters more than lives.'

'No, he hasn't actually said that,' she replied but, as Slaughter blew a smoke ring and watched it drift across the murky interior of the dingy cabin, he wondered if it had ever crossed her mind that her husband might well have the same cynical philosophy.

'Sure, we'll see you safe back to the bosom of your happy household,' he drawled, not without a touch of sarcasm. 'How long you been married, by the way?'

'Not long,' she replied.

'Any sign of children on the horizon?'

'Oh, my God, do I have to listen to any more of his insolence? Can you lend me a spare horse? I can find my own way to San Lorenzo from here. I'll follow the track.'

'Aw, no. We couldn't let you do that. Haven't you noticed? There's some nasty men around out in these parts.'

The advent of much-needed copper cases for bullets meant that the metal could command almost the same price as silver. Big Bucks Clayton had not been slow to see the business opportunity. When an old desert rat prospector had led him to this gaunt canyon miles from anywhere in what was described on maps as 'Uninhabited Region', Bucks was quick to make a claim, raise shares by advertising in the eastern states, and persuade the Southern California Railroad Company to extend their line south-east from Tucson.

Copperolis Canyon certainly wasn't uninhabited now. The mountainside had been torn open to reveal the irridescent green and blue of the copper that lay beneath the rocks. As Slaughter, Snipe and Mrs Hagerty emerged from the mining office they could hear the muffled roar of explosions and the steady pounding of a steam-driven stamp mill.

Clayton was making big money and paying top wages to his miners. Anywhere there was cash flowing a crowd of hungry human vultures swarmed aiming to get some of the pickings. Copperolis was no exception. A ramshackle collection of stores, a blacksmith's and livery, had grown up.

'Aaron's offered to lend you his new hoss,' Slaughter said, offering his cupped hands to Jane Hagerty to help her mount. 'So you won't have to hang on to my sweaty body no more.'

'That's very kind of him,' she called when she was safely in the saddle.

'Ain't exactly kindness,' Slaughter quipped, as he swung on to his own mustang. 'He'd rather head for yonder cantina and cathouse.'

'Memories of the Devil.' Jane read the words scrawled above the door of the flat-roofed, plank-walled establishment as they passed. 'What a curious name.'

21

'Yeah?' He led the way splashing through a copper-streaked stream, through the other shacks and adobes and tents. 'Waal, if you'd spent the night drinking mescal in that joint you'd sure have memories of the devil.'

'Thus speaks one who knows.'

'I've had my share,' he said. 'But I ain't exactly a slave to the cactus juice like some fellers. I can take it or leave it.'

They followed the rail track extension back to where it joined the main track. 'Ain't far now. About ten miles.'

She noticed that he rode with the natural grace of his Indian forebears, as if horse and man were one, whereas Jane went bouncing and bumping along, intent mainly on staying in the saddle and on her steed.

Slaughter had fallen silent, scanning the apparently empty horizon of the scarpland which took on a rosy glow as the sun lowered in the west, setting the sky alight in a blaze of crimson.

She was not to know that this area south of the Gila River and alongside the new frontier, established after the US–Mexican war when vast tracts of territory were surrendered, was one of the most dangerous places in the West. It was the haunt of Apache tribes who still regarded it as their homeland. Many a traveller had been surprised when a savage war party drifted into view as if out of

22

nowhere. Most had not lived to tell the tale.

'The cat got your tongue?' she asked, mockingly, as he paused to peer into the sunset tugging his leather hat down over his brow.

'Nope,' he snapped. 'I got other thangs to think of than small talk. C'mon.'

The Yumas, Pimas and Maricopas were peaceful enough at present but he had heard that young Chiricahua braves had left the reservation and were on the prowl looking for trouble. Why worry her? Even if there was a possibility she might lose her lovely hair. Bands of vicious Mexican bandits haunted this harsh mountain area, too. Real ones. Not like that murderous bunch they had just had a run-in with. The brands on these mustangs enforced the impression they were *Americanos*. But where had they come from? And who, he wondered, was the leader of that callous bunch?

As night fell he was more than relieved to reach San Lorenzo del Rio, right in the heart of this desolate region. The small village established centuries before as part of the Mexican empire had suddenly seen an influx of settlers and a thriving community had seemingly sprung up overnight. Partly it traded with the copper mines, but many of the new arrivals were farmers and small ranchers keen to claim slices of the valuable prairie for themselves.

The huge mission church, raised on the backs of

slaves by the Conquistadors, out of proportion to the adobe hovels clustered at its base, now had a rival. The white settlers had built a main street of stores and false-fronted timber edifices and had not been slow to add a white-painted Baptist church at the far end. Of course, it was nowhere near the height of the crumbling Catholic mission, but when its small bell tower clanged out on Sundays it announced that a new order had arrived.

'So, ye've built yourselves a new prayer house, have you?' Slaughter muttered, as they cantered along the last part of the track.

'Yes,' she replied, proudly. 'My husband was behind that.'

'Yeah, wherever there's church-builders there's hypocrites.'

'Do you have to be so insulting all the time?'

They passed the railroad terminal, devoid of any locomotive, as it would be for quite a while. In the welcome cool of the darkening evening the sky was pricking alight with a firmament of stars.

He grinned as he pulled in his mustang outside the San Lorenzo Hotel. 'It jest comes natural, I guess.'

He helped her dismount, holding up his arms to catch her by the waist. But, as she tried to break away, he held her tight. 'There's one thang that does interest me. Where ya been off to? Sure, I know, it's none of my business.'

'No, it's not.' She hesitated, not struggling to break free as he held on to her. 'I've been to visit my family in California. Have you any objection?'

'Yeah.' He lowered his voice. 'I'd like to know why your husband let you travel on a train that, as mayor of this burg, he must've known was carrying valuable booty and might well be attacked.'

'How would he know that? That's the mine-company's business. Anyway, he didn't know I was taking that train. I didn't cable him until just before I boarded.'

'Why? Were you in two minds about it?'

'You ask too many questions.' She raised a hand, brushing her hair from her eyes. 'Gracious! What a sight I must look, my clothes all torn and dusty, smelling like a horse.'

'You look an' smell OK to me.'

For the first time she laughed at him, her white teeth flashing in the moonlight. 'Well, you should know. You're used to smelling like that.'

'This is where you stay, ain't it?'

'We have a suite here, yes. My husband's in the process of building us a *hacienda* outside town.'

'A *hacienda*? Whoo! Quite the lady of the manor ye'll be.'

'You know, Lieutenant, I sometimes get the impression you're jealous of Mr Hagerty.' She laughed gaily, broke away, and climbed the steps to the hotel. On the sidewalk she paused. 'Come on in and meet Joe. Don't be shy – to use your own words.'

Slaughter loose-hitched the broncs and somewhat reluctantly followed. 'Hell, what am I gittin' into now?' he muttered.

The San Lorenzo Hotel was an imposing two-storey establishment raised out of the dust with pinewood hauled from the mountains. The lower floor was a bar-room and gaming joint, the green baize tables generally occupied and the roulette wheel spinning into the early hours. But tonight there was a babble of voices. When Slaughter stepped inside he was met by a weeping woman in a long dress and sunbonnet who beseeched him, 'Have you any more news? Is my husband alive or dead?'

He recognized her as a lady who ran the haberdashery, her husband holding his dentist's surgery behind the shop. 'He ain't gonna be pulling any more teeth, ma'am, I'm sorry to say.'

It seemed a Mexican shepherd had witnessed the attack from his eyrie up on a mountain top and had wasted no time, once the bandits were gone, in getting on his burro and heading back along the track. He had arrived just a half-hour before Slaughter and Jane.

'Nobody alive,' he repeated. 'All dead. Meester Hancock, the rancher, I see heem. Bullet' – he tapped his forehead – 'in here. Bill Henderson, from Henderson's dry goods. He gone, too. Others, they strangers, most go to work at mines, I theenk.'

'This is an outrage,' a voice boomed, and Slaughter looked across the heads to see a tall, handsome man he knew by sight and reputation as Joe Hagerty. 'We should organize a posse immediately to go in pursuit.'

'It's too late for that,' Slaughter replied surlily. 'They'll have covered their tracks by now.'

Hagerty had his arm around Jane, and she put in, 'This is James Slaughter. He and his comrade fought valiantly. They saved my life. I fear we were the only ones who got out.'

'In that case, sir, I am in your debt.' Hagerty stepped forward to offer his hand to Slaughter. 'I have been in agony this past half-hour not knowing whether my dear wife was alive or dead.'

Slaughter gave him a nod. Their hands gripping was almost like a test of strength. Then he turned to the *peon*. 'Did you see which way they went?'

'*Sí, señor.* They loaded up their dead, about four bodies, I theenk, and headed north-east towards the Basin.'

'Did you recognize any of these Mexicans?' Hagerty demanded. 'Had you seen them in the vicinity before?'

The shepherd squeezed his straw hat in his hands. 'They not Mexican, *señor*.'

'He's probably just saying that to protect his own

kind.' The town sheriff, Ron Cripps, was tall, too, wearing a tin star on his chest. He had a fuzz of babyish hair, and was renowned for taking the easy option. 'Seems obvious to me this was a bad bunch of *bandidos* from over the border. Unfortunately it's way out of my jurisdiction. We ought to contact Fort Apache or the county sheriff.'

'This man's telling the truth.' Slaughter had to raise his voice above the hubbub of jabbering folks and those trying to comfort the sobbing widows. 'They were no Mexicans.'

'Why, if this man arrived half an hour before you, riding on his burro, did it take you so long on horseback?' Hagerty demanded.

'I called in at Copperolis first to report to Buck Clayton. I was head of security on that train. Or I was s'posed to be.'

'Ha!' Hagerty snorted. 'You certainly didn't make a very good job of it. You call that security?'

'I ain't proud,' Slaughter muttered. 'They took us by surprise.'

'Really, Joe, there was no more Mr Slaughter could do. It was bedlam. We were totally outnumbered and exposed. Bullets were whistling; men were dying. It was horrible. I thought it was my last day on earth. I tell you, he saved my life.'

'In that case, sir, I'll buy you a drink and offer you the hospitality of my hotel for the night.' Elegantly attired in a striped suit, with a silk waistcoat and cravat, Hagerty beckoned towards the bar. 'What's it to be? You probably need a stiff un.'

'Bourbon's my preference. I've had my fill of mescal.' Slaughter took the tumbler of spirit that was offered him and swilled it down in one gulp. He glanced at Jane Hagerty and smiled faintly, thinking of what he'd like to give her. 'Thanks but no thanks for the offer of a room. I generally sleep with my horse, as your wife knows.'

'What do you mean?' Hagerty asked, indignantly.

'Oh, Mr Slaughter has a waggish sense of humour. I was rather rude about his appearance and manners.'

'So?' Hagerty demanded. 'Where were you when this attack commenced?'

'As a matter of fact I was talking to your wife.' Slaughter was amused to see Jane's pale cheeks become suffused by an embarrassed blush. 'Goodnight, folks.'

'What—?' he heard Hagerty loudly demanding, as he made his way to the door.

He chuckled to himself as he unhitched the horses. 'Nuthin' like putting the fox among the chickens.'

THREE

It wasn't that he had anything in particular against Hagerty: Slaughter just didn't like his type, that was all. One of those big, brash, patronizing, know-it-all men who impose their views by talking louder than the rest and cold-shoulder any who don't agree. That was probably how he got to be mayor of this town.

'It ain't that he's rich an' powerful and *I* ain't,' he told the mustangs as he settled them into their stalls. 'Nor that he's got a mighty sexy-lookin' wife. Jealous? What me? Of him? Nah!'

He grinned as he saw the ostler in the livery barn listening. 'I must git outa the habit of talkin' to hosses. It's from being out in the wilds so long.'

Slaughter sauntered out into the night. Yeah, maybe she had a point. He sniffed at himself. He didn't smell too sweet. He had visited San Lorenzo del Rio before and recalled there was an excellent bath-house somewhere in the backstreets of the Mexican part.

'It's been a bad day,' he muttered, as he stepped naked into a big half-barrel of warm suds and the girl began to scrub his back. 'A massacre. Death. Blood. Destruction .A ten-thousand-dollar payroll lost. All my men killed, not to mention those other poor devils. A useful locomotive outa action probably for good. Ouch! Take it easy. I ain't a goddamn hoss.'

Sometimes it seemed he had been fighting all his adult life, leaving his young bride and New Mexico home at the age of eighteen to go do his bit in the Civil War. At first it had seemed like fun, joining a bunch of wild cavaliers, Morgan's Raiders, making forays into Kentucky behind enemy lines, blowing up bridges and railroads, looting towns, halting the Yankee advance. But after Shiloh there had been the retreats, the defeats. Memphis lost, Vicksburg lost, until all was lost and the South surrendered.

It was then he had teamed-up with Aaron Snipe, a runty cavalryman from a Tennessee brigade. No, they didn't intend taking the oath of allegiance. They had headed across the border and joined the full-blood Indian, Benito Juarez, leader of the fight for freedom against the French occupiers of Mexico. L'il Benito was president now. It had been nice, for once, to be on the winning side.

'You like?' The girl's fingers slipping enticingly

31

brought him sharply back to the present. 'That nice?'

'Yeah,' he groaned, slipping down into the suds. 'It sho' is. You got a nice touch.'

She was just a bath-house whore. But, somehow, her black hair, her dark lucent eyes reminded him of his dead wife, of those insane moments when he returned to his New Mexico ranch, carved forever in his soul. No, he didn't want to think of *her*. He stroked the *cholla*'s hair. There was no stopping her now. He gritted his teeth and screwed up his eyes . . . why was it the image of Jane Hagerty came into his mind?

After his bath the girl had offered to launder his jeans and long johns, so he strolled out in loose-fitting Mex pyjamas she lent him. He had a meal in a smoky little dive in the Mex quarter, knocked back a few tequilas and was strolling towards the livery when he heard harsh words coming from the open window of one of the rooms above the San Lorenzo casino. 'Why did you come back?' a man's loud voice demanded. 'God only knows!' a woman shrilled. Jane Hagerty stepped through a French door out on to the hotel balcony. Swathed in a diaphanous negligée she stood gripping the handrail, staring out into the night with a look of intense fury.

Suddenly she spotted Slaughter in his odd garb down in the street. He tipped his hat and flicked his fingers in cynical greeting. She stared at him for moments, turned on her heel and went back inside.

'It's bin a kinda exhaustin' day so I guess I'll git me an early night,' he informed the horses as he stretched out on his soogans and saddle beside them in the straw. 'Night, boys.'

But, as he was drifting off, he heard footsteps and, peering through the slats of the stall, he saw the shadowy figure of Hagerty collect a dun stallion, quickly saddle, mount it and ride off into the night.

'Guess he musta got a fancy piece out in the sticks someplace,' he muttered. 'Or maybe not.'

It was the first light of dawn when Hagerty returned, waking Slaughter from his slumber. Again he watched unnoticed as Joe Hagerty returned the stallion to its stall. He made off back in the direction of the hotel.

'Strange,' Slaughter muttered, and went across to take a look at the stallion.

'Whoo! You sure are sweated up, aincha, boy? You musta had one hell of a ride. The bastard ain't even bothered to rub you down. Guess I better do that for ya.'

Later that morning he took a look in the sheriff's office and asked to see the list of stolen or strayed brands. 'What you wanna know fer?' Cripps whined.

'Because I do and I got a right to.'

He had ridden into Mexico City with Juarez and his victorious generals after two years of fighting as the French scuttled from the country like rats deserting a sinking ship. He had returned to the States and spent a year or more as a bounty hunter, so he was accustomed to dealing with surly and supicious law officers.

The sheriff reluctantly produced the list from a drawer.

'This ought to be posted up.'

'Go to hell,' Cripps sneered.

Both mustangs had a knotted rope brand. Two such were posted as stolen from a ranch north of San Lorenzo near Mesquite about fifty miles away. It was just a hunch but maybe the murdering train robbers had a hideout between those two points. It would be like looking for a needle in a haystack but perhaps he should try.

'Thanks,' he said, tossing the list back at Cripps.

When he had dosed himself with strong black coffee in a *cantina* he saw the sheriff heading for the San Lorenzo Hotel. Slaughter followed, but as he approached the hotel, a farmer came charging in on his four-wheel wagon and hauled in outside. He looked mighty hot under the collar as he jumped down and hurried into the casino.

Slaughter slipped unobtrusively in behind him. There were about a dozen early drinkers there, mostly ranged along the handsome mahogany bar. The man who had had it imported all the way from St Louis, Joe Hagerty, had one boot up on the brass foot-rail and was leaning forward talking to the lanky Sheriff Cripps.

The old galoot who had arrived on the wagon, Herbert Warrenburg by name, spotted him and was weaving forward through the chairs and tables. He wore baggy pants, a collarless shirt, waistcoat and slouch hat, the regular garb in these parts. Around his waist was a stout belt into which was tucked a Colt revolver.

'Hagerty,' he cried in a reedy screech, 'what the hell you think you're doin' pulling my stakes?'

The mayor turned to glance at him. 'Me? What are you talking about?'

'Your men.' The wiry little farmer's face was haggard and lined by years of work and worry. He didn't look the gunfighting sort. But Slaughter had the feeling he'd buckled on his gun for some purpose and it wasn't gonna be a cosy chit-chat. 'They just rode up and pulled 'em.'

A man's stakes, of course, were sacrosanct, the way in which he marked out the acres he had claimed, as good as a fence or a ditch. No wonder Warrenburg was in a paddy. Hagerty had barely deigned to turn to him, but now he did so.

'You ain't made the improvements required by Homestead Law,' he boomed. 'So I'm claiming it.'

'What?' Herbert Warrenburg could hardly speak he was so incensed. 'I've sweated and struggled to clear that ground. I've done all a man can do. You keep your hands off my claim. You're a stinking, lousy thief, thass all y'are.'

'Them's fightin' words, Herb,' one of the men at bar remarked, as they began to back away for safety.

'That's what I'm gonna do,' Herbert screched. 'Fight him.'

'You're welcome to fight me in the land tribunal court at Tucson, my friend,' Hagerty drawled. 'I hope you've got a nifty mouth-piece.'

'How can I afford to go to law?' the farmer screamed. 'I can hardly afford to feed my family. But I'll fight you.'

Warrenburg was trying to drag out his revolver from his belt. Not the most expert of gunmen. 'Draw, you varmint. For God's sake! Yes, I'll fight you.'

He had the Colt out, his finger on the trigger and Hagerty was flinching backwards. Slaughter saw a movement of Cripps's arm and there was the crash and flash of an explosion. Warrenburg went back-stepping, cartwheeled over a table, and lay gasping on the floor, his face aghast. He hadn't managed to get in a shot. Cripps ambled over, extended his arm and put another slug in him at point-blank range, finishing the job. He calmly raised his smoking revolver and blew down the barrel. 'Y'all saw what happened. He tried to kill Mayor Hagerty. I had to step in.'

'Why don't you let Hagerty fight his own battles?'

At the far end of the bar Doc Winterhalter was perched on a barstool nursing a whiskey glass. 'That was legalized murder.'

'I don't carry a gun.' Hagerty opened his suit to reveal he was unarmed. 'Everybody knows that.'

'You don't have to,' Doc spat out. 'You have your lackeys do your murdering for you.'

Hagerty turned to him and scowled. 'You better shut your drunken mouth, Doc. Or find another drinking hole. You ain't welcome here making remarks like that.'

'No?' Winterhalter spluttered back the last of his whiskey. 'Why? Don't you like the truth?'

Slaughter noticed that Jane Hagerty had stepped out from a room on to the balcony that led to the wide staircase and was listening intently.

'Why don't you get this ol' fool carried over to the morgue, Doc, and certify him dead?' Sheriff Cripps drawled. 'Otherwise I may have to inform the commissioners you ain't up to the job, you juicehead.'

James Slaughter had seen and heard enough and quietly left the casino as folks arrived to find out what the shooting was. He pushed through them and went along to the mining store.

'Howdy.' He flashed his enscrolled pass as head of security at the copper mine. It had no legal say-so but it was pretty impressive. 'I'd like to ask if you've sold any large orders of gunpowder recently?'

'Let's take a look at my book,' the proprietor mumbled. 'Nothing spectacular 'cept six barrels a month ago to Cass Heron.'

'Who's he?'

'He's been doing some blasting for Mr Hagerty out at the big new house he's building. Blasting through solid rock, I believe.'

'Yeah, right. Thanks.' Slaughter came from the store, scratching at his unshaven jaw. 'Interestin'.'

'Gimme a shave.' Slaughter stepped into the barber shop and took the vacant chair. 'Before this stubble turns into a beard.'

The barber had lathered him and was sharpening his razor on a strop when Doc Winterhalter arrived. 'Why, James, my boy, how ya doin'? What brings you back to this sorry town?'

'Howdy, Doc. What's so sorry about it?'

Of German descent, Winterhalter was a stout, middle-aged man. 'Ach. That man Hagerty's taken us over. He's just had poor old Herbert Warrenburg gunned down. What are his widder and kids gonna do now?'

'I was there,' Slaughter mumbled, as the barber began scraping at his jaws. 'Seemed to me like the sheriff had the right to step in.'

'Ach, *ja*!' Winterhalter took a silver hip flask from his pocket and took a swig. 'Legally they're both covered.'

'Well, you cain't say Herb didn't kinda ask for it. An' you oughta be a bit more careful about the way you spout off, Doc.'

'Hagerty won't have me put down. He might need my professional services one of these days. Somebody with a grudge might get in a shot at him. And there's plenty with a grudge.'

'Why so? A man has to be sharp in business.'

'Not this sharp.' Doc made a cutting motion of thumb across throat. 'Ach! Hagerty's been busy buying up small claims. Those who don't want to sell kinda get persuaded to move on by his bully boys.'

'Yeah? Why should he be so interested in buying up small claims?'

'That, my boy, is a mystery to me. He's obviously got some information we're not privy to.'

'Waal, he's got a mighty handsome wife, that's for sure.'

'Jane? Yes, she's a beauty, ain't she? Swedish descent. He went on a trip to California and brought her back with him. She swishes around in satins and bows like his pet poodle on a leash.' The florid-faced Winterhalter took another swig and lowered his voice. 'Rumour is things ain't so huggy-wuggy in their household.'

Slaughter laughed as the barber finished his job. 'And you wouldn't be one to spread gossip, would you, Doc?'

'How about this?' The barber held up the crow-black strands of Slaughter's thick black hair that hung down from a centre parting almost to his shoulders. 'You need a trim?'

'What?' He stepped from the chair and pulled off the robe, wiping his jaws. 'You cut a Comanche's hair you take away his strength. Forget it.'

Winterhalter roared with laughter. 'You ain't a real half-breed, James, are you? I thought that was just talk.'

'Nope. I'm a quarter-breed. My granny was raped by a Comanche warrior as she crossed the plains in a covered wagon. Me, I've allus bin grateful to that red feller fur letting her live. If you see what I mean.'

He gave a wide grin and flipped a quarter to the barber. 'Your turn, Doc. Man in your position's got to keep hisself spruce. Time for short back and sides. Be seein' ya.'

'You still in the bounty-hunting business, James?' Winterhalter called, in his guttural accent.

'Nope. It ain't bounty I'm after this time.'

At the bath-house he found his jeans, long johns and socks nicely sun-dried, so he pulled them on and buckled his gunbelt.

'Thanks, Dolores,' he called, spinning her a silver dollar.

'*Señor!*' The Latino girl caught hold of his arm. 'I

must warn you. The sheriff and two *hombres* were in here. I hear them say you ask too many question. Beware, *señor*. I theenk they plan to ambush you.'

'Yeah?' He grinned, scoffingly, and patted her backside. 'Waal, they're welcome to try. So long, sweetheart. See ya sometime.'

'*Vaya con Dios,*' she called.

'Yeah,' he said. 'You too.'

FOUR

Hagerty's *hacienda* was in the final stages of construction, built of rock and adobe in a three-sided-shape with a central courtyard, more like a low-slung fort than a house. Slaughter hitched his bronc out of sight among a clump of cottonwoods and climbed up to the natural platform of earth, a fine defensive position on which it stood. He climbed over a stone wall and looked around. At one end some labourers were busy tiling the pitched roof.

A bullet whistled past his head, nicking his ear and, as the sound of the rifle shot echoed away, a voice from behind him rang out, 'OK, hold it. Freeze! 'Less you want the next slug through your brain, if you got one.'

'Yeah,' Slaughter admitted. 'I guess it was a pretty dumb move on my part.'

'I saw you coming a mile away. What you want here?'

'Nuthin' much.' The ex-lieutenant put up his fingers and touched his right ear. Blood was dripping from the lobe. If there was much lobe left. 'Just interested in how you were getting on.'

'What's happening, Cass?' a man asked, as he joined him.

'Who is this creep?' another said.

'Seems like the snooper we been hearing about. Get his gun. Stay where you are, mister. Don't turn round.'

'Yeah,' a gruff voice warned. 'Don't try anythang.'

'Why? Ain't I allowed to see who's gonna kill me?'

'Shuddup.' A pair of hefty, hairy arms grabbed him from behind in a bearhug, and the other man jerked his Schofield away from its holster. 'Right, we got him.'

'Not yet you ain't,' Slaughter grunted, hurling the big bruiser over his head to hit the dust.

Almost simultaneously he spun, kicking out his boot in a high chop to his other assailant's throat. He collapsed, choking, the Schofield spinning from his hand.

'What the—!' Cass fired his rifle again, aiming to kill.

With the agility of a Comanche, Slaughter rolled aside as the slug spat over his head. He came up with a scalping knife in his hand and hurled it on

43

one knee. It thudded into the rifleman's chest. Slaughter was up in a trice, wresting the weapon from his hands, and assisting its owner to the ground with an elbow jab. Cass lay there wriggling and gasping like a speared fish.

Slaughter had no time to waste on him for the big hairy bear of a man was struggling to his feet, going for his six-gun. Without hesitation Slaughter levered the rifle and cut him down.

'You gonna kill me, too?' croaked the third man, on his knees.

Slaughter's face was impassive as he pressed the rifle barrel to his forehead and clacked in another bullet. 'Not if you answer some questions. I want the truth.'

The Mexican builders had come to see what was going on. 'It's OK,' he said. 'The reception party got a little outa hand. It's all over. Me and this fella are just gonna have a li'l chat.'

He turned to them, threateningly. 'Go on. Get back to your work.' He went over and collected his Schofield. 'Creep, eh? Who's the creep now?' he asked the man who was still on his hands and knees. 'OK, start talking. You three were with the gang who attacked the train, weren't you?'

'No, I swear I weren't. Mr Hagerty hired us to guard this place. That's all I know.'

'You were there. I recognize that scar across ya face, in spite of your Mex clothes. You were only fifty

SHOOT-OUT AT SAN LORENZO

yards away. You killed all those people in cold blood.'

'No, please, I beg of you,' the man stuttered. 'I wasn't there. You've got it wrong.'

'Come on. Don't git me mad.' Slaughter prodded him hard in the side with the rifle. 'Hagerty was behind it, wasn't he?'

'No.' The man gasped as the rifle thudded into him again. 'I don't know what you're talking about. That's crazy. Mr Hagerty wouldn't do that.'

'Who was the tall one in the mask, the one with the machete? Where is it they hide out? Come on, I don't want to have to kill you.'

'I don't know nuthin'.' The man stared up at him, like some beseeching old dog, the left side of his face bullet scarred. 'I got kids to support. I'm just doing this for the cash.'

Slaughter pulled the man's wallet from his hip pocket, rifled through it with one hand. No sign of any new, crisp notes, pay-off from the raid. 'Waal,' he drawled and booted him up the rump. 'He don't pay you much, does he?'

He was tempted to put a slug in him and have done with it. It would be the wise move. But he was unsure. 'Maybe I'm barking up the wrong tree,' he muttered, as he turned away. 'Maybe he's telling the truth.'

He climbed over the wall and went back to the mustang the way he had come, taking the rifle with him. It was the 1866 Winchester, an improvement on Ben Henry's model, or so he'd heard. Basically the same, but lighter and a more efficient action. Might come in handy. He didn't want anyone taking a potshot at him as he rode away.

Slaughter had been planning to hang around the livery after dark to see if Hagerty set off on another of his midnight rides and, if so, to follow him. But it was unlikely he would do the same on successive nights. And as soon as the scar-face creep delivered news of his colleagues' sad departures there would be a neck-tie party after him.

'Guess I've played my cards wrong,' he said. 'I'll pick up the other mustang and head back to Copperolis to see what's going on.' He spurred the mustang away. 'Yeah, come on, boy. That's what we'll do.'

Elias 'Scarface' Cooper arrived in a lather at the San Lorenzo Hotel, leaping from his horse and rushing into the casino. 'He's kilt 'em both,' he screamed. 'Cass an' Amos. Shot 'em down in cold blood.'

'Who has?' Joe Hagerty demanded.

'That stone-faced 'breed. The one you warned us about. He come nosin' around. All we did was ask him what he was doin'?'

'You let him get away?'

'Couldn't stop him,' Scarface stammered. 'He's fast and he's dangerous. He's tricky, he is.'

'You damned fool. Go get the sheriff. You're going after him. Don't just stand there.' He jerked a thumb at two surly-looking barmen-bouncers who hung around the casino. 'Go with him. His name's Slaughter. Get him. Understand?'

'What's going on?' Jane Hagerty asked, as she came from their room, her long dress of purple satin swishing against her petticoats and silk stockings as she descended the stairs. A scent of mimosa drifted about her. To most of the riff-raff in the bar who watched she had the air of the unattainable, far beyond them.

'Your wonderful friend, the ex-reb, the knight in shining armour who rescued a lady in distress, has shown his true colours.' Hagerty gave a sarcastic laugh as he stood at the bar and poured himself a stiff bourbon. 'He's killed Amos and Cass at the house. They gave him no provocation.'

'What?' she exclaimed. 'But why? Why should he do that?'

'Because human life means that much to him.' Hagerty snapped his fingers. 'He's a dyed-in-the-wool killer. I've sent the sheriff after him.'

'I can't believe he would do that. They must have—'

'For God's sake, darling! Can't you get it in your head? The man's a vicious murderer. He even killed his own wife.'

'How do you know that?'

'Through the cactus telegraph you could say.' Hagerty took a gulp of his bourbon, more rattled than he cared to admit. 'It seems like when he got back after four years of killing in the war he found his young bride in bed with a Yankee officer. It was too much for his pride. He put a bullet in them both. When two fellow officers tracked him down he killed them, too. He then spent two years as a mercenary in Mexico. When he returned he put his skills to use as a bounty hunter, killing men for a handful of gold. The man reeks of blood.'

'I— He seemed a decent sort of man to me.'

'Doc Winterhalter tells me he's a quarter-Comanche. It's in his blood to kill. He's a mad dog, Jane. He's got to be put down.'

'Aren't you going to put him on trial? Give him a chance to defend himself?'

'Oh, sure, we'll give him a quick trial. Then hang him.'

'God! What an awful country this is.'

'It's the frontier, Jane. It's every man for himself.'

'So much greed, cheating, killing, such a desolate place, heat, dust, flies, ignorance, drunkeness, cruelty. You're a hard man, Joe. Why did I ever come back?'

'Maybe because you like spending my cash.'

'No,' she murmured. 'I thought we could make a go of it. But you're as hard as rock. You'll never change.'

48

'OK,' he hissed. 'That's enough. Don't tell the whole damn town. Why don't you go after your killer friend if you're so enamoured of him?'

'Don't be a fool, Joe. I just thought—'

'Yeah, I could tell what you thought when he was here. I could see it in your eyes.' Hagerty glowered at her. 'Could it be my holier-than-thou precious wife has been playing the whore behind my back with that piece of frontier scum?'

'Don't be absurd, Joe,' she protested. 'He made a few insolent remarks, but I ignored him, put him in his place. It was only when we got here I realized I owed him a debt of gratitude.'

'You did, did you?' Hagerty's fingers dug in deep to her upper arm as he propelled her to the foot of the stairs and he lowered his voice. 'Listen, Jane, get this in your head: you are my wife, for better or worse, and you better get used to that fact. There's no way you'll ever leave me or this territory without my say so again. So I suggest you get back upstairs and keep your nose outa things. OK?'

He kept the mustangs going at a fast lope, leaping from one to the other after seven miles or so to keep them fresh, for he knew they would be after him. As he gained the higher ground and saw Copper Canyon looming up, he relaxed for now he was on Big Bucks Clayton's turf and he had a low tolerance of interfering locals, especially of Sheriff

Cripps's kind. He would back any of his men with the necessary firepower. That's if he still was one of his men?

'What are you doing back here, Slaughter?' Clayton bellowed, as he sat behind his desk. 'You ain't on my payroll no more. Get out. And take that runt of a sidekick with you. He's been drunk as a rat's arse for two days. Mescal's blown his reason away.'

'Aw, Aaron cain't help it. He's had an unhappy, lonesome life. Sometimes he needs to forget. I guess we all do at times.'

'Lonesome? He don't look very lonesome. He's like a friggin' ferret trying to fornicate with every Mex piece in the camp. He won't even leave the grannies alone. I've had complaints. Get the hell outa here, both of you.'

'Come on, Buck,' Slaughter drawled. 'Whadda ya want? We did our best. I'm still working on the case.'

'Best ain't good enough. Call yourself security men? Pah!' He jabbed a stubby finger at Slaughter. 'You're fired. *Adios*!'

'What about my three hundred bucks?'

'Go sing for it.' Clayton pondered the specifications for a new shaft. 'I'm busy.'

'Look, Buck, it ain't just the cash. It's a matter of pride to me. And Aaron, too.' Slaughter sat on the desk corner and reached to help himself to a

Havana cigar, but Clayton snapped the humidor shut. 'I wanna catch up with these jokers. I don't like falling down on a job. Look, I've got a proposition for you.'

'Oh, yeah,' Clayton sighed wearily. 'Just what would that be?'

'How about if I get your payroll back you give me a quarter share?'

'You *look*, Slaughter.' Big Bucks stood and prodded him in the chest. 'That cash weren't just payroll. It was all I had to cover all kinda expenses to keep this mine rolling. You can have an eighth share.'

'Make it a sixth and we're talking,' Slaughter said. 'That's only a thousand bucks or so 'tween Aaron and me.'

'You're on.' Clayton's pugilistic face split into a grin. 'Here, have a cigar.' He had an idea Slaughter's arithmetic wasn't as accurate as his shooting. If he got any cash back he could easily twist him with the pay-out.

'Right, here's a contract I wrote out. Just put your signature there.'

'Jeez, you think of everything. Doncha trust me?'

'I don't trust nobody.' Slaughter tucked the contract in his pocket and lit up. 'How about we go celebrate 'fore Snipe drinks the bars dry?'

'So howdya plan earning your dough?' Clayton asked, as he knocked back a tumbler of railroad gin.

51

'My main suspect was Hagerty.'

'Joe Hagerty? What's he got to do with it?'

'Maybe I'm wrong. Maybe I just don't like him.'

'Not on account of his wife, perchance? Maybe she's clouded your judgement. Joe's a cold-hearted grasper, but that don't make him our man.'

'So, OK, I'll concentrate on finding the blue-eyed jasper.' Slaughter had avoided the spirituous liquors. He tipped a steam beer to his throat. It was cooled with mountain ice but it tasted like rusty rainwater. 'I suggest me and Snipe go back to the train crash site and fan out, look for their hideout in the back hills. These guys might scatter like the 'Pache after a hit, but they must meet up again someplace.'

'Right, I've gotta go out inspect the damage to the engine and the track. The Southern California are sending two men out tomorrow to see what can be salvaged. We'll leave first light.'

Just then Aaron lurched through the bead curtain of the doorway of Memories of the Devil supported by two Mexican ladies of the night. One was extremely fat and oily; the other as skinny as a starved rat and minus most of her teeth. The little Snipe had his arms around their shoulders. 'Why, hiya, Lootenant,' he slurred. 'You been missin' all the fun. Meet my fiancées. We jest got engaged.'

Slaughter and Big Bucks glanced at each other, stood up as one, took hold of Aaron and hoisted him outside. 'Time for you to sober up,' Slaughter said. 'We got work to do.' Together they pitched the little Snipe head first into a corrugated iron barrel of rainwater. 'This is probably what they make the beer outa. Might improve the taste.' Aaron was dragged out spluttering and plunged in twice again, his legs kicking. They dragged him along to the livery. 'You got a busy day tomorrow,' Clayton said. 'Sweet dreams.' He slugged him in the jaw and, as Aaron collapsed they pitched him into the straw beside the mustangs.

'Let's hope he sleeps it off,' Slaughter drawled. 'Mescal ain't easy to escape from once it's got its fangs into a man.'

'Where were we?' Big Bucks asked, as they returned to the cantina. 'Oh, yeah, it's your round.'

FIVE

The railroad officials had arrived on a small locomotive which had been left, its engine idling, back along the track. They were bustling about making notes on checkboards. Slaughter was standing beside a row of unmarked graves of the unknown dead as Big Bucks came bustling past, chomping on a cigar.

'What's the verdict?'

The mine boss tugged at the tight collar around his bulging neck. 'Purty good. The cow catcher was mangled but took the brunt of the collision as the engine turned over and ploughed into the rocks. They're gonna bring in heavy lifting equipment. They figure it can be repaired and put back on the track.'

'The van looks like its had it. They musta blown the safe sky high.'

'Yeah, but the wheels and bed of the passenger

carriage are basically OK. They can easily build a new one of wood. It wasn't exactly a Pullman, was it?'

'About as comfortable as a cattle truck.'

'The good news for me is that the company wants to take over the running of the track. When I wanted them to lay a line out here I had to chip in part of the cost, plus rental of the engine. They've offered to pay me back in full and the company will be sole operator from now on.'

'Why, I wonder,' Slaughter queried, 'should they do that?'

'I dunno, pal,' Big Bucks said. 'But it takes a weight off my shoulders. It's been costing me a whack to keep this line open.'

'So, how long before they're back in business?'

'I dunno. Maybe a month, maybe two. Until then goods for the mine and San Lorenzo will have to be hauled in along the old wagon road.'

Slaughter beckoned Snipe over. 'Time we set to work seeking that cash. There's about fifty square miles of ravines, scrub and desert. I'll go to the west, you go east. We should aim to meet up in three days' time at Apache Hole. OK?'

'Sure.' Aaron sat the other mustang, glumly.

'How's your head?'

'Pounding like a damn steam hammer.'

'Give up the cactus juice. Stick to a decent tipple like bourbon or gin.'

'Cain't afford it.'

'Slaughter!' Big Bucks mangled boxer features split into a grin. 'You sound like some ol' spinster lecturing her wayward son.'

'Yeah, well that's what I feel like sometimes with him.' The former lieutenant swung on to his own, if stolen, mustang. 'C'mon. Let's go.'

'By the way,' Big Bucks shouted, 'the other good news is those stolen bills were all fresh minted. We've got the serial numbers so they can be easily checked.'

Slaughter nudged the mustang with his knee and circled back. 'They're probably deposited in a bank over in Mexico by now.'

'Nah, that wouldn't be a wise move. A Mex bank could go bust any time. President Juarez has inherited millions in foreign debt,' the mine owner opined. 'You'll find our cash, pal. I'm relying on you.'

They climbed their horses up to the rim of the scarp. The train robbers' tracks were plentiful. But soon, as expected, they began to disperse, until eventually there was little sign at all on the sunbaked rocks.

'This is where we split up,' Slaughter said. 'If you ain't arrived by high noon I'll head on for Mesquite. If you git in any trouble fire off three shots. OK, Aaron?'

'Yes, suh, Lootenant.' The wiry Snipe saluted

fingers to his faded Confederate forage cap. 'High
noon. Not tomorrow. The next day. I gotcha.' He
tugged at his reins and cast away. 'Best of luck!'

'Yeah, we'll need it,' Slaughter muttered as he
pushed on into the unknown and the sun's rays
hammered down.

For two days he had zig-zagged back and forth
through wind-eroded rocks and ravines. A grey and
purple desert basin stretched before him as the
crimson ball of sun melted behind the Indians'
sacred Boboquivari peak amid the distant mountain
ranges. There were no trails, no sign of life except
for an eagle spiralling on hot air currents high in
the clear sky. No smoke. No drifting dust. 'If they
got a hideout round here it sure is well-concealed,'
he muttered.

It was time to make camp and he chose a corner
of rocks alongside a ravine of saguaros. He doled
out a hatful of his precious water to the horse, gave
him a handful of split corn and hobbled him so he
could graze on whatever nourishment he could find
among the thorns. He lit a small fire. The saguaros
would disperse his smoke. But he glanced around
nervously. In this hostile country a man never knew
when Apaches might appear. He boiled up coffee in
his battered pot and supped the brew thoughtfully.
A big chuckawalla lizard sat on a rock and watched
him. Other creatures, rattlers, prairie foxes,

kangaroo rats, and the big, rarely seen Gila monster, would have lain all day under the rocks out of the heat. Soon they would emerge into the night. There was a huge lonesome silence out here. It made him feel like he was the last man on the planet.

Therefore, as he reached for a can of tomatoes and an opener, it was a considerable shock to hear a man's gruff call. 'Hallo, the camp!' It was an odd, educated Eastern voice, by no means a frontiersman's, that came again. 'Can I come in?'

Slaughter's mug of coffee went flying as he grabbed up his Spencer and levered a slug into the breech, down on one knee, an instinctive response to danger.

He listened, peering warily into the shadows of saguaros which stood with their prickly limbs raised as if in supplication. But he could make out no one.

When the question was repeated he called, 'Show yourself, mister. Come forward if you're a friend.'

It was an even odder sight that appeared coming out of the saguaros. A tall, well-built gentleman of ruddy countenance wearing a solar topee and off-white canvas suit, leading a mule and holding a rifle in one hand. 'Good evening, sir,' he greeted.

'Where'n hell did you come from?' Slaughter growled. 'You made me jump outa my skin creepin' up like that. I didn't hear a damn sound.' He shook out his coffee-damp leg. 'Nearly scalded my marital prospects.'

His visitor ground-hitched his mule, gave a deep chuckle, and squatted down cross-legged on the far side of the fire. 'Sorry about that but one has to be a tad careful in this sort of country.'

'Help yaself to cawfee,' Slaughter drawled, settling himself back against his saddle and indicating the pot.

'No, thank you. I don't take stimulants of any kind. Plain water does me.' The gent removed his helmet to reveal a balding brow and scratched at his mutton chop whiskers. He produced a big jack-rabbit and began to skin it. 'Perhaps I can avail myself of your fire?'

'Sure, why not? But . . . I ain't heard no shot.'

'No, I snared the poor thing. Can't risk a shot. It gives the jolly old game away, what?'

After he had gutted the animal and hid the evidence well away under a rock, the stranger busied himself finding dry firewood and attending to his mule. 'Always look after one's animals,' he said, 'and they'll look after you.'

'Exactly my sentiments,' Slaughter muttered, as he watched his companion skewer the rabbit with a greenwood stick and prop it over the glowing coals.

'Hope you don't mind my joining you.' The gent propped his rifle to one side and pulled out a revolver from inside his crumpled suit. He laid it nearby on a rock. 'Nice to have a bit of company, but not everyone's fond of it.'

'You're welcome,' Slaughter remarked producing his pouch of tobacco makings and offering it. 'Fancy a smoke?'

'No thanks. I find it affects one's sense of smell, always an advantage in these parts.'

'You mean you can sniff out the 'Pache?' Slaughter's stone-still face split into the grooves around a grin. 'Waal, I guess that's a possibility. Seen any sign of any on your travels, pal?'

'No, I'm sorry to say not.'

'Sorry?'

'Yes, perhaps I should inform you I'm with the army.'

'Blue-bellies?' Yankee soldiers were not Slaughter's favourite cup of tea. 'Where's your company?'

'Oh, miles behind. I thought I'd have a scout around on my own. We're after that wily fellow Cochise, I expect you know.'

'Yeah, he's been leading you a merry dance, ain't he? How many troops you got? Three thousand? And you cain't pin down a band of three hundred Apaches?'

'He's a very clever leader. They know every ravine, can live off this unwelcoming land.'

'Yeah, the murdering bastards. But strikes me they got just cause.'

The military man turned the jack which was browning nicely. 'I have heard he was treated unjustly by our troops and has sworn vengeance. But we have to bring him in, of course. Can't have him setting farmsteads to the flames.'

'No, I guess we can't.' Slaughter gave a sardonic cackle. 'Seen any sign of some murdering white men, possibly dressed as phoney Mexicans, on your travels?'

'The train raiders? No. We're after them, too. Could have caused a nasty international incident, but fortunately, like you, we saw through their ruse. What's your interest, sir?'

'I'm working for the mine company. We want our cash back. I had a hunch they might have headed this way. But seems I'm wrong.'

'Would you care to join me?' The visitor pulled the rabbit from the spit, broke off a leg and offered it. 'I do believe it's done.'

'Thanks. Have some of my tomatoes and beans.'

'Don't mind if I do.' The gent held up the other leg. 'Look at the muscle on that. These jokers can go at forty-five miles an hour and leap fifteen feet.'

'You don't say?' Slaughter mused. 'Very tasty.'

When he woke in the early dawn his companion was reviving the embers of the fire, feeding in some sticks. 'Good morning. You look the sort who goes in for breakfast so I've put your coffee pot on,' he announced in his hearty way.

'Ain't you having none?'

'A mug of cold water and hardtack biscuit is good

61

enough for me.'

'Yeah?' Slaughter growled, as he filled his tin mug with scalding black coffee and spooned in sugar. He sat on a rock and revived himself. 'That head-piece you got on – that the latest fashion?'

'Not exactly. But they're ideal in this baking heat. It was a hundred and ten on the Fahrenheit scale yesterday. All the British have them out in India. Pith helmets they call 'em.'

'Yeah? 'Spect they're ideal fer pith-ing in, too.' He guffawed like a mule at his joke. 'Ye'll be telling me next that damn mule of yourn is the ideal form of transport.'

'Certainly. I'd back it any day against a mustang for staying power in this kind of country.'

'I doubt that, but I ain't gonna put it to the test.'

Slaughter took another sip of his coffee and studied the gent. 'I got a feelin' I seen you some place afore.'

'Possibly you saw my photograph splashed in one of the rags. I've recently taken over the Department of Arizona. The name's George Crook.'

'Gen'ral Crook?'

'Yes, you've got it. I didn't catch yours.'

'That's 'cause I didn't give it. James Slaughter. Fought aginst you blue-bellies in the recent l'il Misunderstanding 'Tween the States. My ma was convinced I'd be a general when I rode off. But I only made lootenant. Guess I weren't cut out fer it.'

'Really. Who with?'

'Morgan's Raiders. The First Tennessee Cavalry.'

'Morgan? That old rogue. We called you lot The Forty Thieves. All the looting you used to do.'

'Yeah. We didn't go short of much.'

The general stood ramrod straight, took a small brass telescope from his jacket pocket, put it to his eye and scanned the landscape. From this eyrie at about 2,000 feet they could see for miles. 'I fear Cochise is miles away causing mischief somewhere. You may criticize our army, but regulations only allow us to push our plugs thirty miles a day. Yon Apache, as no doubt you know, scorn horseback in this sort of country. They can run seventy miles a day with ease.'

'So that's why you ain't caught 'em yet?'

'We will. Don't worry.' Crook put the 'scope away and picked up his rifle. 'I'm heading back to find my platoon. How about you?'

'I'll ride along with ya for a bit.' Slaughter untied his mustang. 'When I hit the wagon road I've gotta go up to Mesquite to return two stolen broncs to their rightful owner.'

They rode for three hours in silence, Crook holding his heavy rifle in his hand like an Indian. No wonder the Apaches called him Grey Wolf. Suddenly, as they were descending a ravine, he pulled in his mule and hissed, 'What's that?'

Slaughter jerked out his Spencer from the saddle

boot, snapped a slug into the breech, ready for battle. But he could see no sign of trouble. 'What?'

'Up there.' The general was putting his telescope to his eye again. 'If I'm not mistaken it's a Swainson's hawk.'

'Swainson? Who the hell's he?' Slaughter croaked, somewhat rattled.

'The man who named it. Fancy seeing that so far south.'

Crook regarded Slaughter balefully. 'You know, I really can't understand you settlers. You seem to have no interest in your area's natural history. How can you be so unobservant? Why, this morning I've noted pigmy nuthatches, painted redstarts and, would you believe it, a beautiful parulid.'

'Parulid?'

'Yes, a red-faced warbler in the woods up there. Didn't you see it?'

'No, I don't believe I did.'

'Surely you've noticed the cactus wrens in the saguaro trees? Such industrious little creatures, pecking about among the needles, keeping the tree clean.'

'Wrens? In the soo-aros. Yeah, I've seen them. Is that what they're doing?'

'Yes, some of the saguaros are dying from a nasty black rot, *cactobrosis fernaldialisis*,' the general explained, airily. 'Larva of a moth that burrows into the flesh and introduces a bacterium. However, we

64

must press on. There's a waterhole not far ahead. We can stop for a spot of luncheon.'

'Yeah,' Slaughter grinned. 'That'll be nice.'

Jeez, he thought. This sure is some general.

At high noon they reached Apache Hole and Crook said he was going to fire shots to alert his platoon which he believed was not far away. He went off into the scrub at a crouch, and while Slaughter chewed on a strip of jerky he heard the gun reports barrelling away along the valley. The bushy-whiskered general returned beaming, a brace of quail dangling from his hand. 'Got two on the wing with two shots. Missed the third,' he said.

'You don't say,' Slaughter replied, quite impressed.

'Allow me to present them to you for your supper. Your company has been most amenable. Aha, I hear their approach.'

Sure enough there was a thudding of hoofs and jingle of harness and his platoon of cavalry appeared. The dark-blue uniforms of most of then were faded and ragged, their boots caked with mud, their faces burned by sun and wind, their hair and beards uncut and wild. Some wore colourful variations of the regulation, fringed leather coats, or campaign hats decorated with feathers or headbands. They had obviously been out on the trail a long while. On foot with them were two half-naked Apache scouts. A young lieutenant, clean-shaven, his uniform almost new, aide-de-camp to the general, protested, 'Really, sir, I've been worried sick wondering where you were.'

'Don't fuss, Fortescue,' Crook snapped as the men watered their horses.

'Well, we must be off now.' He turned his mule away, then paused. 'Oh, by the way, Slaughter, forgot to tell you. Spotted a Mexican chicadee yesterday.'

'Yeah, I've come across a few of them myself in my time, General,' Slaughter grinned widely. 'So long y'all.'

Ten minutes later Snipe came riding in. 'Heard the shots. Thought you might be in trouble, Lootenant.'

'Nah, it was just some ol' general potting us quail. Find anythang?'

'No, not a sausage.'

'Never mind, my friend. We'll just keep on looking,' Slaughter said. 'Relax, Corporal. First we're gonna cook up these quail for – what did he call it? – luncheon.'

SIX

'Them's my hosses,' the gnarled old rancher hooted.

'Good,' Slaughter said, as they rode into his yard. 'Hear tell you're offerin' a reward.'

'Where'd you find 'em?'

'We took 'em off them who stole 'em.'

'What happened to the thievin' rascals?'

'I do believe they've gone to meet their Maker.'

'Hell. They weren't bad boys; just misled.' He inspected the two mustangs, and took a worn wallet from his pocket, extracting four even wearier-looking five-dollar bills. 'Twenty dollars. That's what I said. Thanks, boys.'

Slaughter stepped down, accepted the cash. They were good mustangs, sound in lungs and limb. He dug out another ten. 'Tell you what, we'll give you thirty for these moth-eaten thangs. We need to git back to San Lorenzo. That's fair, ain't it, Aaron?'

Snipe made a downturned grimace. 'Aw, no, that's too much, Loo-tenant.'

'Done', the rancher said, snatching the cash and tucking it back in his wallet.

'Who were they?' Slaughter asked, as he remounted. 'The ones who stole them?'

'Dell Simms and Danny Sniveley. Lazy coupla young coyotes. Told me they'd been offered another job that would pay bigtime. Next thang I knew they were gawn. On my hosses.'

'Any idea who they planned to work for?' Aaron asked.

'No, but I did see 'em talkin' to some feller the day before. He rode up to the bunkhouse door, offered them this job outa the blue. Got some damn nerve.'

'A tall man with vivid blue eyes?' Slaughter suggested.

'You got him.'

'Not yet we ain't. But if you can think of anythang else about him we possibly might.'

'Not really,' the rancher mused. 'He had on a brown frock coat, bootstring tie, fancy vest, like a gambler. Sharp, clean-shaven features, a black moustache.'

'For *not really*, that's purty good,' Slaughter said.

As Slaughter was turning his mustang away, the rancher called out, 'Oh, yeah, when that character took off his hat, I remember now, he was completely bald, 'cept for a bit round the sides.'

As they rode away Aaron yelped, 'If he'd taken one of them new-fangled photygraphs we couldn't have had a better description.'

'True,' Slaughter said. 'Now all we gotta do is find him. It sounds like this character was riding around ranches recruiting deadbeats to do his dirty work.'

'Yep,' Aaron agreed. 'Dell and Danny didn't know what they was gittin' into.'

Darkness was fast falling by now. Mesquite didn't have much to offer. It was just a collection of shanties and adobes scattered both sides of the trail; aptly named, for it sat mid-centre of a flat stretch of thorn and mesquite. But when they saw a sign swinging in the desert wind saying 'Beds and Eats' they decided to book in.

It was a lopsided little house of paint-peeling shiplap boards, two up and two down, as they say. A white fence protected a weedy yard and at the back was a tumbledown stable, a shed and privy.

'These are the accommodations,' Mrs Maggie McLeuclar announced in her shrill Scots accent as she opened up the musty shed to reveal a couple of iron cots. Ye can light yon candlestick. But dinna let it burn too long. Wax candles don't grow on trees, ye know.'

Slaughter and Snipe stabled the mustangs, threw them a tin pail of oats and some alfalfa, dumped their saddles and panniers on the bunks, punched dust from the pillows and stained mattresses and eyed each other.

'Guess it ain't the Ritz,' Slaughter said, easing off his boots and socks and soaking his feet in a bucket of water. 'But it'll do.'

'When did she say the eats would be ready? In an hour?' Aaron propped his Ben Henry against the wall. 'We got time to go grab a beer first?'

'No, we ain't. You're on the wagon, Corporal. That's an order.'

'Let's go chivvy-up the wrinkled old hag then. I'm starving.'

'No need to be disrespectful. She's a poor widder lady.'

Maggie McLeuclar was pounding her gnarled fists into a knob of dough on a floured board. 'Ye needn't expect your dinner yet. I wasn't expectin' company. Ye can stoke the stove for me.'

Slaughter had discarded his buckskin jacket and chaps and was in just his jeans, faded vest, barefoot, his Schofield slung across his loins, black hair hung about his monolithic features. It was pleasant to sit on a stool and watch the old woman at work. Reminded him of the mother and home he once had.

The widow kneaded the dough into shapes and put it in the big iron stove to bake. 'What do you want, man?' she asked as she stirred oatmeal in a pan. 'Pies or pig's-trotters?'

She poured the porridge into two cracked bowls, spooned in molasses. 'Here, ye can be having this to be getting on with. Pies it'll be.'

A while later, after they had feasted on her pork pies, scooping up the juice with hunks of warm bread and Slaughter was just stuffing the last piece of jellied crust in his mouth, there was a shout from outside.

'Come out with ya hands high. The house is surrounded.'

'Heavens!' Maggie McLeuclar screeched.

'Shee-it!' Slaughter let out a hiss of anger at their folly. 'They've caught us with our pants down.'

Aaron had made a dive for the back door by the stairhead and peeped out. 'Hell, they've cornered our longarms. There's one of 'em on the roof and one in the shed.'

'You hear us in there?' a voice thundered. 'Toss out your guns and step outside. I'm counting to ten then we start shooting.'

'Wait!' Slaughter caught hold of the widow's arm as she started for the front door. 'I'll warn them you're coming out.'

'Oh, what devil's schemes have ye brought with ye?' she screeched, struggling away. 'Take back your three dollars for the beds. Be out of my house.'

'We cain't go out,' he said. 'They'll hang us.'

'No doubt a well-deserved fate,' Maggie scowled.

71

'What mischief have ye done?'

'It's a long story,' Slaughter growled. 'Stay there while I parley.'

He climbed the narrow stairs two at a time and poked his revolver out of the open window of the front bedroom. In the half-darkness he could see the lanky Cripps standing behind a handcart he had pushed forwards for protection. He took a bead on his head with the Schofield but hesitated. 'The lady's coming out,' he shouted. 'Let her through safe.'

'What about you?' Sheriff Cripps called.

'Ye'll find out,' Slaughter muttered. He shouted downstairs, 'Open the front door nice 'n easy, wave a towel or somethang, then step outside.'

He watched her walk towards the sheriff, giving him a piece of her mind. She was pushed to one side and shadowy shapes of men began to close in.

'What's it to be?' Cripps yelled.

'Go to hell,' he growled, and the revolver kicked in his grip as he tripped the hammer and blasted out a bullet. Cripps's Stetson was sent flying. 'That was just a warning.'

'Let 'em have it, boys,' Cripps cried, ducking down.

Carbines, shotguns, revolvers rattled out their message of death in a furious fusillade, peppering the woodwork, smashing the windows, sending splinters flying. All Slaughter could do was hit the floor and hold tight. When there was a sudden lull he was up on one knee and returning the leaden compliments, but he was only able to take wild shots before dodging back as another hail of bullets smashed whining through the thin walls.

Aaron was letting loose his own volleys with his handgun through the downstairs back window. Slaughter dodged into the back bedroom and aimed his last and sixth cartridge at the man on the shed roof. 'Got you,' he growled, as the fellow's arm jerked back and he dropped his rifle.

He started to reload from the dozen copper cartridges in his belt as Aaron came pounding up the stairs. 'I'm all out of lead, Lootenant,' he shouted as he skidded to a halt beside him. 'I weren't expectin' this.'

'Nor me. We're getting careless in our old age, Aaron. Help yourself from my belt.' He cocked his Schofield and peered outside. So they now had six bullets each. 'If we could reach the stable we could make a break on the hosses. We need to get that one inside the bunkhouse and get our longarms an' ammo.'

He fired, smashing the shed window. But he knew it was a forlorn hope. This was confirmed by a flash of gunfire from the shed and a bullet nearly took off his nose. Five slugs left.

'I'll keep 'em busy at the front. You watch the back.'

From the front window he aimed two more precious bullets, but was unable to dispatch Cripps or any of his shadowy henchmen. Suddenly he saw that they were lighting tar flares. As one was about to be hurled Slaughter desperately fired at the thrower who collapsed with a bullet in his thigh.

'We gotta git out, Aaron. They're gonna burn us down.'

Snipe was on the stairhead and their eyes met amid the flash of gunfire. Aaron gave a toothy grin and tugged his forage cap down. 'Aw, well, we cain't win 'em all, Lootenant. We've had some high old times.'

'Come on.' Slaughter jumped down the stairs and charged out of the back door, making a beeline for the bunkhouse, firing as he went. If he could get to his carbine. . . .

Suddenly there was an ominous click. The Schofield was empty. And, as suddenly, several men had hurled themselves upon him, and although he wriggled and fought like a wildcat they were too much for him. Soon he was pummelled and trussed as tight as a spider's fly, a noose tossed around his neck and pulled tight. He was swung around and could see that Aaron had suffered the same fate.

'Waal, whadda ya know?' The weak-chinned Sheriff Cripps was standing before him. 'If it ain't our friend Slaughter. He don't look so dangerous now.'

'Get lost,' he growled.

Cripps booted him without warning in the groin.

Slaughter grimaced, gasped and hissed out, 'I'm gonna remember that.'

'Yeah, I guess y'are,' Cripps jeered, as the rough-looking *hombres* around him laughed. 'You can remember it in half an hour when we hang ya.'

'What have ye done to my house?' Mrs McLeuclar was wailing, but Cripps pushed her aside as they dragged Slaughter and Snipe to the stable, put them on their mustangs.

'Get outa my way, you old witch.'

There were about twenty men in the posse, three of them wounded in the affray. The latter were being helped on to their mounts as they all prepared to move off, when there was the thudding of hoofs, and the clatter of sabres. Who should hove into sight but General Crook and his platoon of ragged cavalry.

'What's going on?' Crook demanded as he held up his hand to bring his column to a halt and drew up his mule in front of them. He spotted Slaughter and Snipe sat on their mustangs amid the bunch, ropes tight around their necks. 'Don't tell me it's a lynch party.'

'No, suh. No way.' Cripps nudged his horse forward, pointed to the tin star on his shirt. 'I'm the sheriff of San Lorenzo. These men are dangerous criminals. They've been arrested for several

75

homicides, plus horse theft. We're escorting them back to our town for trial. All these men are my sworn-in deputies.'

'Is that so?' The general gave a somewhat contemptuous snort. 'Well, I only have your word for it. And to tell the truth, by the look of those ropes around their throats, I suspect that their chances of getting to San Lorenzo alive are somewhat slim. Sheriff, you should not be condoning a lynch party. Remove the offending objects immediately. I intend to look further into this.'

'I'm going to sue him for the damage he's done.' Mrs McLeuclar was waggling her finger at the sheriff and screeching, 'He's no goin' to get away with this.'

'Yes, madam, indeed, you have every right.' Crook saluted her. 'Might I avail myself of your premises to investigate?'

'Ye're welcome.'

'Right, Sergeant,' the general called out. 'Detain all of these men. Lieutenant, find my writing materials and come to the house. I'm holding a judicial enquiry. Bring in the two defendants. Sheriff, here's your chance to put your case. You may present any reliable witnesses.'

'Who the hail you think y'are, ordering us about?' Cripps replied, in an aggrieved nasal whine. 'You ain't got no authority over me.'

Crook eyed him severely. 'I have every right as United States general in charge of the south-western sector. This is a war zone and martial law applies. Follow me, Sheriff Cripps.'

As he swung from his mule the general barked out, 'Trooper, bring in the colours.' He added *sotto voce* to a corporal, 'Escort the lady over to a neighbour's. I don't want her interrupting me.'

A bullet-scarred table was righted. Crook sat behind it on a stool, the flag of the Third Cavalry held high beside him. He removed his pith helmet. 'Let's get to the bottom of this. Present your case, Sheriff.'

'That man's a homicidal maniac.' Cripps pointed a finger at Slaughter. 'He illegally entered a building site in San Lorenzo by climbing over a back wall when there was a notice clearly marked, "Trespassers will be shot". He was ordered to halt by Cass Heron. He did so but when two other guards caught hold of him he wrassled free by some kinda Chinese ju-jitsu, chopped Elias Cooper in the throat, tossed Amos Sutton over his head, killed Cass with his scalping knife, and shot Amos dead.'

'For a start,' Slaughter butted in, pointing to the scabbed remains of his ear lobe. 'Heron didn't just say stop. He did this.'

'You'll get your chance to speak. Wait your turn.' Crook said. 'What happened next, Sheriff?'

'He stole a hundred dollar Winchester and

escaped after torturing poor Elias almost to death. We raised a posse and have been scouring the country for five days. When we rode in here tonight we was told that him and his sidekick was hidin' out in the Scotch woman's house. We called on 'em to surrender but they opened fire badly injuring three of our men. When they ran outa lead we caught 'em.'

The general asked, 'Have you any witnesses?'

'Only Elias. T'other two's dead.'

'Call him.'

Elias Cooper was handed the general's personal Bible and swore to tell the truth. He nervously stroked the white bullet scar across his cheek and gave a similar account.

'He held me down, beat me, kicked me and tried to make me confess I was one of them murdering train robbers. I would have none of it.'

'Were you?' Crook asked.

'No, 'course not.'

Sheriff Cripps concluded, 'When Slaughter come into San Lorenzo I noticed he had two stolen mustangs. That's the second charge.'

'Let's hear your version, Mr Slaughter.'

'Sure.' Slaughter eased himself away from a bullet-holed wall, and drawled, 'It was like this. As security officer of the Copperolis Mine I had reason to suspect Joe Hagerty of nefarious activities.'

'Hang on,' Crook said, 'who's he?'

'That lowdown rattlesnake who runs San Lorenzo town. He's got that piece of shit the sheriff and, I wouldn't mind betting, most of them thugs outside on his payroll.'

'Avoid the libellous and incendiary remarks,' Crook barked out, tugging at his luxuriant mutton chop whiskers. 'Nor do I approve of bad language. Does your case harm. And pause between sentences, Lt Fortescue needs to get all this down.'

'True I got over the wall at Hagerty's place. I wanted to see what he'd got there. True I killed two men but it was in self-defence when they shot at me. Sure, I gave Scarface a boot up the backside. I took the Winchester in case he tried to shoot me in the back. He can have it back if he wants.'

'What else?' Crook asked.

'Oh, yeah.' Slaughter took a crumpled bill of sale for the two mustangs from his jeans pocket. 'Me an' Snipe here ain't no hoss thieves. That's a damnable lie. We didn't surrender just now 'cause we knew that lousy skunk Cripps and his gang would hang us if we did.'

He stood barefoot, disarmed, and grinned, 'If you find us not guilty, Gen'ral, I'd like my Schofield returned.'

Crook jutted his prow of nose at Snipe. 'What about you? Anything to say?'

'Nope,' Aaron replied. 'The Loo-tenant's said it all. But I don't s'pose we'll git no justice from you lousy stinkin' blue-bellies.'

'*Au contraire*,' Crook announced. 'In fact, I have come to the conclusion that firstly Sheriff Cripps has not proved his case, and secondly, under the law of *habeas corpus* he has no right to hold these two men in custody. Also he has no business being here for Mesquite is well beyond his legal juristiction. Therefore the charges are dismissed. The sheriff must return their personal property. And I order him to leave this town with his men and return to San Lorenzo post haste. Thank you.'

Fortescue jumped to his feet, clicked his heels and saluted, quill pen in hand. 'Emergency court session closed. Make way for the general.'

SEVEN

Jane Hagerty had a basket of shopping over her arm, fresh produce from the market stalls chosen for the hotel kitchen. She was casually dressed in a Mexican cotton blouse, loose skirt which revealed her bare ankles, rope-soled *huaches*, and a straw sunhat from which her golden hair coiled down about her shoulders. She strolled in the shadow of the towering mission church and spotted a Papago woman, a blanket about her shoulders, from which a baby's head, with auburn hair, protruded. The mother was squatting by the church door begging.

'Hello,' Jane said, kneeling to stroke the child's bright locks. 'What a beautiful baby. Did his father have red hair?'

'I dunno.' The woman's dark eyes were expressionless. 'He didn' take off his hat.'

'Good Lord!' Jane gave a gulp of horror when she saw that the woman's nose had been sliced off and was a festering scabby mess. 'What happened to you?'

'My tribe throw me out. I got nowhere to go.'

'Oh, dear.' Jane pressed a silver dollar in her hand and hurried across to the Hotel San Lorenzo. As she entered the casino she heard her husband's voice raised in anger.

'You telling me you let 'em get away again?' he bellowed at Sheriff Cripps. 'You had 'em sat on hosses with ropes round their necks an' you gave 'em up?'

'I cain't argue with a US gen'ral, Joe. That's what he ordered us to do.'

'*That's what he ordered us to do,*' Hagerty mimicked. 'You sadsack. What are you, a damn girl? You fall down on a job again, Cripps, an' you can get the hell outa this town.'

'What about some cash up front, Joe?' Cripps whined. 'When you going to divvy up?'

'When the time's right.' Hagerty was standing at the bar and had not noticed his wife. 'I got one more job for you. I'm foreclosing on the Rawlings' property along in the valley. Don't take no arguments. Here's a bill of forfeiture I've had made out. They can't argue with all that legal flapdoodle. If they do, pull their stakes, throw 'em out.'

'What if Rawlings and his sons won't go, Joe?'

Hagerty shrugged. 'You know what to do.'

He turned and started visibly with surprise when

he saw his wife, her vivid blue eyes staring at him. 'What you lookin' at?'

'How can you do that, Joe?' she whispered, hoarsely. 'Throw those poor people out. *Have* you legal authority?'

'Sure I have; they ain't carried out their obligations under the Homestead Act. What's it to do with you? And what you in them clothes for? You look like some damn *peon* wench.'

'What's wrong with that—?' she began to say.

'All right, Cripps, don't stand gawping. You can go.' Hagerty strode across to Jane and brushed his fingers against her blouse, her loaded basket, dismissively. 'What's all this? We got cooks who can do the shopping.'

'I'm sick of being idle all day.' Jane thumped the basket down on a table. 'I'm trying to be of help. And I'm tired of being wrapped up in satins and velvets, buttoned up so tight in this heat, my legs hobbled by a long skirt, looking like something out of an out-of-date fashion plate.'

'You're my wife,' Hagerty shouted. 'You've got a position to uphold. I'm not having you wandering the streets looking like some Mex saloon slut.'

'There's nothing wrong with these clothes.' She, too, raised her voice with exasperation. 'I want to feel free. I can dress up in the evenings for you if it's so necessary.'

'Just do as I say, girl,' he hissed through gritted

teeth. 'I'm too busy to argue with you. I got thangs to do.'

Jane bit her lip as he stalked out of the casino and headed for his land office across the street. How, she wondered, did she get into this marriage? How could she get out of it?

But, after she had taken the shopping into their woman of all work, Maria, she calmed down. Compared to that poor woman along at the church she was, she realized, extremely well off.

Nonetheless, all day the image of the hopeless woman and her orange-haired child worried her. It summoned all the coldness and cruelty there was in this territory towards the original inhabitants on whom had been imposed such an alien culture.

Jane was dressed by her maid in finest satins and silks, a pearl necklace around her throat, gold bracelets and wedding band, her hair coiled up on top and held by a Spanish comb, to dine with her husband, in the casino restaurant that night.

Eventually she broached the subject of the beggar. 'Isn't there something we could do for her and her baby? Can't we take her in, let her help Maria in the kitchen?'

In the flickering light of the ten-candle chandelier above their heads her husband scowled at her as if she were mad. 'That's what the Apache *do* if one of their wimmin has a white man's bastard. They chop off her nose, throw her out. It ain't nice,

I know, but it's the law of them primitive devils. There ain't nuthin' we can do about it, Jane.'

'But, surely, we can't just leave her to starve.'

'That's enough.' Still chewing on his meal, he wiped his mouth, threw his napkin down. 'If you think I'm having some 'Pache squaw and her bastard in my house you're badly mistaken, my lady. You better go up to your room. I got a busy night ahead.'

'What's it say, Nathan?' Old Man Rawlings, his wife and two sons were sat around their kitchen table in the lantern light peering at the notice served on them. 'You've larned your letters. Read it out agin. You couldn't have read it right afore.'

'No, Pa, I read it right. It don't make no sense. It don't real say what we ain't done.' The 18-year-old youth brushed his fair hair from his eyes and read the foreclosure notice again. 'It's all double talk, ain't it? Legal mumbo jumbo.'

'Let's have a look,' his 16-year-old brother, Jethro, cried, snatching at it. But after a bit he gave up. 'Cain't make head or tail. Says we ain't got no right of appeal.'

'Sheriff Cripps said we gotta be outa here by midnight tonight.' Mrs Rawlings's thin hair was pulled back severely from her haggard face, her long, dowdy dress buttoned tight to the throat. She peered around the low-roofed timber cabin. 'How

85

can we do that? We got the hogs an' chickens to load on the wagon. What we gonna do with all the other stuff, leave it behind?'

'Where we gonna go?' Jethro demanded.

'We ain't goin' nowhere,' Rawlings announced. 'It's a bluff. That pig Hagerty just wants to get his greedy hands on our land.'

'He seemed mighty pleased to sell it to us,' his wife said. 'Why should he want it back so bad?'

'Hell knows,' Rawlings replied. 'Anybody'd think there was a seam of gold runnin' under our land.'

'That's crazy,' Nathan scoffed. 'This ol' bit of land ain't no use to nobody. Why, we can barely scratch a living from it ourselves.'

'I don't like it.' Mrs Rawlings voice trembled as she looked at their old clock. 'Four hours to go. You think they'll be back tonight, try to force us off?'

'Sheriff Cripps wouldn't allow that,' Rawlings said. 'I'll go see Hagerty in the morning. I'll tell him iffen he gives us back what we paid for it then we'll go.'

'What?' Jethro jeered. 'This land's worth more'n you paid for it, Pa. What about all the work we done?'

'We ain't going.' Nathan stood up and reached for the sporting rifle he used to kill critters. 'They ain't running us out. I'll sit on the porch all night and see 'em off if they come. I ain't in no mood to parley.'

His mother gave a squawk of fear. 'Don't be a fool, Nathan. That ain't the answer.'

'What else can we do, Ma?' Jethro asked. And he, too, went to find his shotgun, an ancient piece all but falling apart, but usable.

Walt Rawlings just sat there, staring at the letter, looking as sick as he felt inside. Occasionally he glanced up at the ticking clock.

James Slaughter and Aaron had tried helping Mrs McLeuclar patch up her damaged house, but there wasn't a lot they could do about the bullet holes in the walls. And she had told them in no uncertain terms to be off. They had brought enough misfortune on her head.

They had headed back towards San Lorenzo, a fifty-mile ride on the wagon road. They assumed the posse would have returned long before, and would have had enough of chasing folk. In any event, they deemed it wise to by-pass the town and, although night had long since fallen, took a semi-circular course around it across open ground. A full moon had arisen casting a silvery sheen all around.

Slaughter had taken the ride at an easy pace, stopping for rests *en route*, and he was confident that although it was getting late, almost midnight, they could cover another fifteen miles to Copperolis. In spite of what Crook thought, a mustang in good fettle had the stamina to go for many miles with little sustenance. And it wasn't rough country.

They were about to join the winding dust trail out of San Lorenzo again when they suddenly saw a bunch of riders going in the same direction. Slaughter quickly pulled in under the dark shade of a big cottonwood. Moonlight shone on a star on the shirt of the leading rider. 'That's Cripps,' he hissed.

'Yeah,' Aaron agreed, as the horseriders went thudding past at a fast clip. 'And his same lousy posse by the look of 'em.'

'They're heading along the Valley. What mischief are they up to tonight?' Slaughter wondered. 'In this light we better let them get ahead or else we'll be spotted.'

Suddenly, as they pounded along the winding trail eating the posse's dust, they saw them turn off to encircle the Rawlings' homestead. There was the sound of gunfire and screams. Some of the riders had lit tar torches and were hurling them at the low timber buildings which were already crackling in flames.

Young Nathan Rawlings had been tensely awaiting the raiders and didn't pause to ask questions as they came charging towards him. He fired his sporting rifle at the leading riders. The first to die was a man called Abe Hunisett who took the bullet between the eyes and toppled from his mount.

Jethro, too, blasted the riders from his position in

the shadow of the barn, giving them the full benefit of both barrels of his shotgun. Three more riders were caught in the spray of lead and tumbled from their horses.

There were howls of fury from the men at being ambushed and they and their horses swirled away in confusion. Nathan took the opportunity from behind his barricade of logs to reload the single shot, and young Jethro delved into his pocket for two more shells.

Walter Rawlings ran from the cabin, a look of horror on his face as he saw the fallen dead and wounded men. He raised his arms, standing between his sons and the men, pleading, 'Stop! For God's sake, no more!'

'You started it!' Sheriff Cripps hollered. 'An' we're gonna finish it.'

'No!' Mrs Rawlings was out on the porch and she ran to stand beside her husband. 'For mercy's sake.'

But there would be no mercy now. The chips were down. Cripps swirled his horse around and led another charge at them, firing his six-gun point blank at Old Man Rawlings who went back-pedalling into a horse trough, his blood curdling the water crimson.

'You bastard!' Jethro hollered and let loose two more barrels, sending horses and riders crashing to the dust in a whinnying tangle of limbs and hoofs.

But they would be the last shots the boy ever fired

for Sheriff Cripps hauled his horse about, charged Jethro, bowling him over, then shot him in the face as he lay on the ground. His mother screamed and ran to kneel over him, gibbering with horror at it all. Her husband and youngest son already gone.

The men ignored her. None wished to be accused of murdering a woman. While some lit more tar torches and sent flames spritzing across the cabin's tinder-dry roof, others sought Nathan, who had leapt from his barricade and sprinted away to find a hiding place behind the hog pens.

It was at this point in the battle that Slaughter and Aaron arrived, the former-guerrilla fighters assessing the situation and charging into the affray without hesitation. Slaughter rode, his knees gripping the mustang's sides, his Spencer poised at shoulder, picking his targets, sending four more attackers into the great oblivion, operating the trigger guard with the ease born of years of fighting, churning out bullets until his seven were spent.

He then twirled the carbine in his hand, stuffed it back into the saddle boot, pulled out his Schofield and rode back and forth in the darkness dispatching even more of the riders to Kingdom Come.

As whining bullets, screams, shouts and flames made the night a holocaust, Aaron stuck by his side on the other mustang, blasting others with his revolver until that, too, was empty. He then dragged out his heavy rifle and swung it like a battleaxe, engaging the incensed raiders in hand-to-hand combat.

From his hidey-hole among the hogs, Nathan added to the slaughter, his single shot flashing, until the remnants of the so-called posse had had enough and set off as fast as they could go, back the way they had come.

Suddenly silence returned. All that could be heard was the groans of the injured, the woman's sobs, and the low insistent roar as the fire took hold and the flames leaped and danced in the night, timbers crashing.

Aaron, after a fight, was always jubilant, and true to his southern hillbilly instincts, began robbing the dead of whatever cash and valuables he could find on them. Or stood and gave the wounded the kiss of death with his revolver.

Nathan ran to join him. 'What are you doing?'

'Showing 'em the same mercy they showed your pa and brother,' Aaron replied, dismissively, as he pressed his gun to another man's forehead, ignored his pleading eyes.

'Anyhow, you cain't trust coyotes like these iffen they got an ounce of breath left in their body.'

Nathan went to haul his dead father from the trough, and to try to console his mother as she sobbed over Jethro's bloody corpse. 'It's over now,' he said.

'It ain't over yet.' Slaughter picked up a tin star from the dust. 'I'm goin' after the man who lost this.'

He vaulted back into the saddle and set off, quirting the mustang to a gallop as he headed back along the trail to San Lorenzo.

Only four of the score of men who arrived at the Rawlings' household had survived. Two of them had had enough and shown the town a clean pair of heels, galloping on in the direction of Mesquite.

San Lorenzo was strangely quiet as Slaughter slowed his mount and trotted in alertly. Only a mandolin was being plucked in one of the *cantinas* in a plangent lament. Most of the town was asleep, although Doc Winterhalter had emerged from a down-at-heel beer parlour, calling out, 'I heard some shootin' down the trail. What's going on?'

Slaughter ignored him and rode up to the front of the San Lorenzo Hotel. A light was flickering inside, the chandelier still burning. 'Come on out, Cripps,' he shouted.

Instead, Joe Hagerty stepped from his casino, and stood on the sidewalk. 'What do you want?' he asked, gruffly.

'I wanna see the owner of this.' Slaughter held up the tin star, which flashed in the moonlight. 'He left it behind when he burned down the Rawlings homestead, when he murdered the unarmed Walt

Rawlings and killed his son, Jethro.'

A few folk, Latino and Anglo, had ventured from their *casas* and shops and listened, hushed by his words.

'No doubt on your orders, Hagerty,' Slaughter shouted. 'You're the one behind all these killings.'

'That's a damn lie. I don't know what you're talking about,' Hagerty protested. 'I've been here all night.'

'I bet you have. While your boys do the dirty work.'

'That's a slanderous statement,' Hagerty shouted. 'As mayor of this town I order you to cease this outrageous disturbance and be on your way. You're the murdering scoundrel, if anybody is.'

Slaughter caught sight of the blonde-haired Jane Hagerty step out on to the balcony in her white nightdress and stand watching and listening.

'Come on, Hagerty, are you too much of a lousy yeller snake to back your lies with gunplay now thangs ain't goin' your way?' Slaughter slipped lithely from his mustang and took a stance about thirty paces from the casino sidewalk. 'Come on, or am I gonna have to take ya with a noose around your neck to Tucson to answer these charges?'

'I am unarmed.' Hagerty opened his smart frock coat to show the watchers that this was true. 'I am no street brawler. I advise you to go away, Mr Slaughter.'

'Yes, I back that.' Sheriff Cripps moved out of the shadows from behind him, the six-gun in his hand blazing. A bullet scorched past Slaughter's cheek as he hoisted the Schofield from the greased holster across his loins. Three times each fired, almost simultaneously, stepping towards each other as they did so. Lead whined and ricocheted. As the fourth shot reverberated, Cripps caught hold of his abdomen, his Colt falling from limp fingers, his eyes fixed as he crumpled, trying to catch hold of Hagerty as he slid to the boards of the sidewalk.

'Now, how about you, Joe?' Slaughter called as their gunsmoke roiled. 'You gonna fight? Or do I take you in?'

'You ain't gonna do nuthin'.' Elias Cooper came from the darkness at the side of the hotel, his carbine barking out. 'Except die.'

It was like a sledgehammer hit Slaughter in the chest, knocking him off his feet, taking the wind out of him, and he groaned with a mixture of shock and anger as he hit the dust. Everything, the houses, the people roundabout, seemed to be moving back and forth, as he jerked up the Schofield in one final effort, thumbing back the hammer and aiming instinctively.

The world started to spin as his bullet hit Scarface Cooper in the chin, speeding upwards to disintegrate his skull in a mess of blood and brains.

'You—' Slaughter began to say as darkness

engulfed him.

Jane ran from the casino, only a dressing gown over her flimsy nightdress, to kneel beside James Slaughter, raising his head from the dust to cradle in her arms. 'Please,' she begged, 'don't die.'

'It's too late,' a hard voice grated out, and she looked up to see her husband standing over him. 'That murderer's got what he deserved. You're wasting your blandishments, you two-timing whore. He's dead.'

Hagerty gave a cold-hearted laugh and turned to go back to the hotel, stepping over the sheriff's body on the sidewalk, and going inside.

There was the thud of a horse's hoofs and Snipe came riding in. The little backwoodsman bounded down to Slaughter's side. 'Who done this to the lootenant?' he asked, drawing his pistol and looking around.

'Scarface Cooper,' Doc said. 'Slaughter took out Cripps and Coop'.'

He nodded across at the bodies oozing blood on to the sidewalk outside the casino. The undertaker had arrived. In his tall Lincoln hat and black suit he was bent over like a vulture, measuring them for coffins.

'Help me carry your friend inside,' Doc said.

EIGHT

'*Ja*! Vairy int-er-resting.' Doc Winterhalter examined the wound in Slaughter's chest through his pince-nez perched on his nose. 'You see, the ball entered here.' He touched the gaping hole with his scalpel. 'It hit a rib and passed through, to be deflected by his shoulder blade, exiting beneath out of his back. Your friend is either lucky or unlucky. I am not sure which yet.'

'He had better be lucky, Doc, or it'll be the worse for you,' Aaron gritted out as he held up the hurricane lamp. 'He won't be paying your bill.'

'*Ja*, there is that to bear in mind.' Winterhalter's German ancestry became more obvious in times of stress. 'Where is my whiskey? Ach, here.' He pulled the cork and tipped the bottle to his lips, taking several good glugs as he contemplated Slaughter's half-naked body. 'I need a shot before I begin. It steadies my shaking hands. How about you?'

'Nah.' Aaron shook his head. 'The lootenant put me on parole. I'm only allowed beer or gin.'

'You have a stronger character than me, if so. Mrs Hagerty, are you ready with the hot water and swabs? We must try to clean the wound, staunch the blood, and sew it up.'

Instead of following her husband back inside the hotel, Jane had helped them carry Slaughter into the doctor's surgery. He lay there now, still unconscious, but breathing deeply. Thank God for that, she thought. In spite of the doleful situation she could not help but be struck by the part-Comanche's magnificent physique as they peeled off his shirt. His chest was hairless and sun-darkened, his ribcage pronounced, every muscle of his abdomen above his narrow waist apparent, his strong arms sinewed and sculpted.

'A fine specimen of a man, eh?' Doc remarked, noting her regard. 'Just look at those pectorals. However, if you would be so good as to thread my needle we will begin.'

She did so with the catgut twine as Winterhalter took the bottle and splashed liquor liberally upon the wound.

'Christ!' Slaughter exploded, one booted leg kicking at the sky, coming to life. 'What the—'

'Language.' Winterhalter waggled his forefinger. 'There's ladies present. Stick his belt 'tween his teeth, Aaron. Hold it there. Bite hard, James, you're going to be all right.'

'Aagh!' Slaughter cried out like a scalded cat again as they turned him over and Winterhalter pointed to the exit hole. 'Take it easy, will ya?' he groaned.

'Don't be such a baby, James,' Jane cooed. 'We're trying to help you.'

'Hold him still,' Doc cried, as he tipped whiskey on the neat hole and took another swig himself. '*Alle guten Geister*! I've earned that.'

Such was the pain Slaughter relapsed into unconsciousness again as they rolled him on to his back. 'I can only hope no bits of bullet or dirt and powder grains were left inside.'

'Do you think he'll pull through?' Mrs Hagerty asked.

'Many shot men die of blood poisoning. But he is as strong as an ox,' Winterhalter said, finishing the bottle. 'We can only hope so.'

'I must go now. My husband is foolishly annoyed with me,' she said. 'He seems to think—'

'Can you blame him?' The doctor smiled at her. 'May I thank you, on the patient's behalf, for your help?'

Her husband was more than annoyed: he was livid. When she opened the door to their suite of rooms he dragged her inside by her blonde hair, smashed her across the face, knocking her to the floor. 'You bitch,' he shouted, whipping off his silver-buckled leather belt, and brandishing it. 'You need to be taught how to behave.'

In the kitchen below Maria bit her lip with fear hearing the belt whistling, Jane's screams. She clutched at her rosary and prayed.

San Lorenzo undertaker, Uriah Levick, rubbed his hands with bright-eyed anticipation as he and his Mexican helper carried the coffins of Sheriff Cripps and Elias Cooper out of his mortuary and loaded them, one on top of the other in his hearse. 'You got the graves dug, Antonio?'

'*Sí, señor.* I work all night.'

'Well, we got to git 'em planted quick in this heat.' Uriah adjusted his crepe-swathed top hat to a more sober angle, and brushed dust from his black frock coat. 'Hear tell there's plenty more stiffies along at the Rawlings' spread. You up to it?'

'*Sí, señor.* I theenk so.'

'Business has sure been looking up lately.' Levick had been quick to have words with the mayor after the shootings. Mr Hagerty had assured him all the corpses who had no known kin could be buried and charged to public funds. The same as he had said after the train was derailed. Levick had got to that site in time to stop the vultures making too much of a breakfast out of them. Antonio had worked all day burying the unknown ones at the spot, and they had transported those with family back to San Lorenzo.

Levick had nothing against the vultures and ravens, they did a good clean-up job, but they sometimes robbed him of his profits if he arrived too late. 'Come, look lively, man,' he urged. 'We've got a busy day.'

The Mexican, in his black cotton suit, scrambled up to the box of the hearse, and Levick clambered arthritically up to join him, as the horses set off towards the cemetery on the hillside. Boot Hill a lot of folks called it, due to the fact that most men around these parts died with their boots on. That seemed to be particularly so recently.

Antonio gave the horses the whip on the way back and the hearse went careering across the rough ground behind the town, in a not very funereal manner, towards the Rawlings' place. Uriah Levick was in a hurry today.

Nathan, his fair hair tousled over his brow, was standing in a woollen vest and dungarees keeping guard over a line of dead men sprawled on the ground. 'I been keepin' the crows away,' he said.

'Ah, yes,' Levick muttered, inspecting them. 'Crows seem to be real partial to the eyes, as you see. Find them a great delicacy, no doubt. Know any of 'em?'

'No, only Abe Hunisett. He's got kin out at Sunset Ridge. He was the first one I killed. Don't know the others, only that I've seen them hanging around the saloons.'

'Aye, the usual frontier scum, drifters who think they're hard men. This is the way they usually end. I guess sacking shrouds will be good enough for them.'

'I'll pay for a coffin for Abe,' Nathan said. 'I guess it's the least I can do.'

'It would be some consolation to his kith and kin,' Uriah agreed. 'Because they're not going to be too pleased with you.'

'What else could we do?' Nathan pleaded. 'They were trying to burn us down.'

'I see they succeeded.' The hunch-backed undertaker glanced at the smouldering remains of the house. 'What are ye going to do now?'

'I've told Ma I'm not leaving. Hagerty will have to kill me, too. We've moved into the barn. Pa and Jethro are laid out in there.'

Mrs Rawlings was in a state of numb shock, kneeling by her husband and son's bodies, whispering prayers to whoever might be listening up in the Great Unknown.

Mr Levick took his measurements and said to Nathan, 'I guess you're the man of the house now. So you'll be in charge of the disbursements. It depends what sort of a funeral you can afford. The best ones don't come cheap, pine boxes, brass handles, all the trimmings, hearse, flowers and I can provide nice headboards.'

'Yes, we'd like the best,' Nathan said. 'Of course.

But we were thinking of burying them here, along by the stream. There's a bit of shade. So we wouldn't need the hearse.'

'Ah, no,' Uriah protested. 'That wouldn't be allowed under the Homestead Act. They need to be interred in hallowed ground. Come, come, boy, you don't want to skimp over your loved ones. They need a proper resting place.'

'Boot Hill,' Nathan muttered, 'don't seem very proper to me.'

'Well, they could go in the old Spanish cemetery. What I'm saying is, have you any cash to put up front? Only I don't want to be wasting my time here. I'm a busy man.'

'How much?'

'I'd like the whole amount,' Uriah muttered, busy jotting down figures in his notebook. 'Only I hate chasing debts. It ain't dignified for a man in my profession.' He pointed to a not inconsiderable sum he had arrived at. 'Could you manage that?'

Nathan's eyes opened wider with surprise. 'Yes, I think so. I found Pa's cash tin. I believe there's enough.'

'Good,' Levick snapped, rubbing his hands once more and chuckling to himself. 'I hate to talk cheap. So, now we can get started.' He sniffed the corpses' ripe aroma. 'Yes, sooner the better.'

Sweat was streaming from Slaughter's body as he

lay, semi-conscious, on the cot in Doc Winterhalter's surgery. Jane Hagerty had called in before noon to see how he was. She was wearing a grey suit, with a grey hat and veil across her eyes. She leaned across the cot and with a damp sponge wiped at his impassive, rutted face, gently pushing back from it the thick, black Indian-esque hair. 'What's this ointment on the wounds?'

'Looks to me like tecole grease,' Snipe said, showing her a can of it. 'Same as what they daub on calves' ears when they jinglebob 'em.'

'He's not an animal,' Jane exclaimed.

'Guess the doc thought iffen it's good for steers it's good enough fer a tough ol' bull like the lootenant.'

'And what's this?' She sniffed at a flask of liquid and a glass on the bedside.'

'He's been giving him a few drops of laudanum. Said it would make him sleep.'

'Laudanum? Goodness, I can't see what good that will do. What else has he prescribed?'

'He took a bottle from a cabinet.' Aaron went to take a look. 'That un', there. What's it say?'

'Brimstone,' Jane read. 'That's an odd remedy for a fever.'

'Aw, Doc's a bit rough and ready, but he knows what he's doing. You don't want to worry about that, Jane. I reckon whiskey's his main remedy.'

Just then they heard the door opening and

Winterhalter returning from his morning shave and trim over at the barber shop. 'Good morning, Mrs Hagerty,' he called. 'Why the veil?'

'It's the fashion,' she replied, somewhat flustered. Doc reached over and lifted the corner. 'You'd better let me dress that eye. You've got a real shiner.'

'It's nothing. An accident. The broomhandle caught me. I tripped.' She winced as she moved on the chair, easing her skirt, uncomfortably. 'I'm wondering—'

'The broom handle didn't whack you across your rear parts, too, did it? Perhaps I should take a look,' he suggested, smiling creepily.

'That won't be necessary. Nor do I think brimstone or tecole grease would do me much good. I must say I'm rather worried about your medical methods, Doctor. Does the lieutenant really need laudanum? Wouldn't it be best to let the wounds heal of their own accord?'

'My dear young lady,' Winterhalter chided, 'brimstone is one of the most important medicines ever discovered for fighting infection. Laudanum is a relaxant. He was tossing and turning so there was a danger of the wounds opening. He's lost too much blood already. Don't you fuss. He's fine.'

'Well, I don't read the latest medical magazines, but—'

'No, of course you don't. In fact, admit it, like

most layfolk you don't know what you're talking about.' Doc held her hand and patted it. 'You just leave the treatment to me, OK? And if I were you I'd put a beefsteak on that eye.'

'I have to go,' she said, extracting her hand from his. 'My husband doesn't approve of my—'

'Joe's been chastizing you, has he?' Winterhalter found his best Kentucky bourbon in the cabinet and poured himself a tumbler. 'A cowardly act, striking a woman. But a man's entitled to beat his wife. You should have known chasing after the lieutenant would enrage him.'

'I didn't chase after him,' she retorted. 'But, I suppose, yes, Joe had good cause to chastize me. I married him and I must go on with him for better or worse.'

'Let's hope,' Aaron said, 'it don't get *too* worse.'

Winterhalter took a good sup of his bourbon. 'Dear madam, I don't wish to interfere,' he said, 'but I think you must realize you married a bad one. Isn't it obvious that your husband is behind those killings last night? He's the one at the top of the pyramid. He's the one who gave orders to the sheriff to clear out the Rawlings.'

'Joe says he didn't have anything to do with it.'

Snipe laughed. 'Waal, he would say that, wouldn't he? I gotta agree with the Doc here, ma'am. That man of yourn is, in my opinion, a lowdown, murderin' snake. James here has strong suspicions

105

he was behind the massacre at the train you, yourself, were involved in.'

'No,' Jane Hagerty exclaimed. 'I can't believe that.'

'You must make your mind up, my dear,' the doc advised, 'whether you believe us or you believe Joe.'

Jane's body seemed to slump as she stood, looking through the veil at them and at the feverish body of Slaughter. 'Joe said that all he told the sheriff to do was to pull their stakes and tell the Rawlings they had to get out. He said the sheriff told him the settlers started it by shooting and killing his men. He had to retaliate.'

'Yuh,' Snipe said. 'So if the sheriff didn't start it why did they charge in there with burning brands in their hands? I saw 'em with my own eyes, Jane.'

'Come, Mrs Hagerty, face facts.' Doc Winterhalter escorted her to the door. 'If you don't believe us perhaps you should eavesdrop on some of Joe's conversations. You're the one nearest to him.'

'Yuh, an' if I was you, ma'am, I'd try taking a look in his safe when you can. Iffen he's got a wad of brand new dollar bills, like thousands of dollars, that'll mean he's guilty.'

'You mean you want me to spy on my own husband?'

'We townspeople just want to know the truth, that's all,' Doc said. 'We've trusted Joe as our mayor, but how much longer can we do that?'

'Oh, dear,' Jane cried, as she stood in the doctor's open doorway and heard the sound of a muffled drum, a slow, insistent beat. 'It's the poor Rawlings family.'

A Mexican in a black suit was leading the procession. The unctuous Levick was on the box of the hearse, holding back the twin greys, who were tossing their black ostrich feathers and stomping their hoofs. Through the hearse's glass sides they could see two coffins beneath piled wreaths. Behind strode Nathan, in his church suit, holding up his distraught mother, followed by a straggle of mourners led by the Revd Ayling, the new baptist minister, holding open his Bible.

Winterhalter stood to attention beside Jane, who noticed her husband come from the saloon, that hard wooden look on his face, as he watched the procession. Jane broke away from Doc's restraining hand and ran across the dusty street to catch up with the mourners, walking along at the rear of the funeral procession as it headed towards the Spanish cemetery.

Winterhalter rubbed his hands as Snipe joined him. 'It looks like she intends to defy him. I hope she's not in for another beating.'

NINE

The tolling of a bell in the high tower of the mission church was one of the few sounds to break the silence of San Lorenzo. The Spanish population, as was their custom, had closed their shops, or come in from their allotments shortly after high noon to take a traditional siesta and shelter through the afternoon from the blazing heat of the day. And many of the new Anglo settlers followed their example. The hotel casino and a couple of smaller bars, however, remained open to do a desultory trade.

Few folk, therefore, noticed the arrival of a lightweight black-painted coach, not the regular stage from Tucson that called once a week, but obviously privately owned. Its four greys came clipping into the wide and dusty main square to do a U-turn, being drawn up by its driver in front of the hotel.

A door was tentatively opened, as six outriders attired in range clothes took stances about it, apparently scanning the houses for any sign of trouble. The first to step out was a Mexican girl in a scarlet dress and golden bracelets, her shining black hair tumbling to her shoulders. Her wanton manner betokened exactly what she was to the gentleman who stepped down behind her.

Like some faithful little mongrel, Aaron Snipe was hanging about the doc's adobe house for he feared another attempt on the lieutenant's life. Or, more precisely, he was lounging at a table and chair beneath the shady forecourt that fronted it. Half-dozing, his forage cap over his eyes, his interest perked up at the sound of the coach. 'Hey, jest git an eyeful of that purty li'l *señorita*.' he cawed to himself. 'Who's this jasper?'

The gent was tall and slim, attired in an earth-brown frock coat trimmed with velvet, his black pants tucked into silver-decorated boots, a wide-brimmed black hat shading his face from the sun. 'If that's his coach he sure ain't short of a bit of cash,' Snipe muttered.

When the man and the girl had climbed the steps to the hotel sidewalk and entered the batwing doors of the casino, two of the outriders stepped down and took positions immediately outside, while another two strolled around the back. Hung with iron, they looked what they were, paid bodyguards and taking no chances.

The coach driver, his shotgun guard, and the other two men busied themselves watering and feeding the horses. Then one snapped his fingers at a *peon* sat on the canopied sidewalk and told him to go fetch a jug of *cerveza* from a nearby *cantina*.

Snipe went back inside, checked on Slaughter, who still seemed to be in a feverish coma, and roughly shook Winterhalter awake from his snores as he lay on a *chaise-longue* in his study.

'Hey, Doc,' Snipe said. 'Somethang funny's goin' on over at the casino.'

'Vot?' The medical man had emigrated to the States from Munich and he came out occasionally with a spluttering of incomprehensible German. 'Who is it?'

'That's what I'd like to know,' Snipe said, uneasily, describing the new arrivals.

Winterhalter tied his cravat, pulled on his jacket, and went outside to take a look.

'Mighty interestin', huh?'

'*Ja.* Sure is.'

'Why don't you stroll over and bluff your way inside, say you're desperate for a bottle of whiskey. They won't take no notice of a lush like you.'

'I don't like it. Those guys look like trouble.' Winterhalter stroked his jaws, considering. 'OK, I'll give it a try, see if I can overhear anything.'

The portly medical man jerked on his homburg,

tugged the brim down over one eye, and ambled over to the casino. Snipe saw him remonstrating with the two guards on the door, heard him laugh and shout, 'Boys, I've got a desperate thirst. I practically live here. It's the only joint where they sell bourbon. Let me through. Ask Joe, if you don't believe me.'

One of the men went inside, reappeared and gave him the nod. 'He's in,' Snipe commented to nobody in particular. 'Good.' He picked up Slaughter's Spencer, eased a slug into the spout, just in case.

Jane Hagerty had been sitting at a table playing patience by herself when the pretty Spanish-looking girl came swishing and sashaying into the casino. A tall gentleman behind her directed her to the bar. He was a sinister-looking cove, a fancy revolver strapped to his thigh beneath his coat, not that that was unusual. He had sharp, hawkish features, burned mahogany by the sun, as was his shiny bald pate, for he tossed his hat on to the bar and greeted her husband like an old friend.

Joe Hagerty was standing behind the bar in shirt sleeves, but as always, immaculate in a tight, satin-backed waistcoat and bow-string tie, silver cuff-links flashing. He reached out a hand to grip the stranger's. 'What's it to be, Mr Black?' he asked.

'A drop of the Kentucky,' Black replied. 'Yeah,

the same for her. She likes to live dangerously.'

The Mexican girl shrieked with laughter, tossing back her shimmering curls, reaching for her glass, and putting a slim arm around her companion's waist.

Jane, interested, stood, straightened her purple dress and strolled over. 'How about one for me?'

'You don't drink this time of day,' Hagerty said, frowning at her. 'This is my wife, Jane.'

'Well, I thought I'd join the party.' She was wearing a patch over one eye. She nodded at Black and was struck by the intensity of his ice-blue eyes. 'Hi.' But a tremor of fear passed through her. Could it be him? The killer with the machete charging along the train track, severing the engineer's head from his body? No, surely not. He seemed too respectable.

The girl was directing a volley of Spanish at her which she only partly understood when a fellow came in and said, 'Some guy called Doc wants a bottle. Shall I let him in?'

'He's harmless,' Joe said, 'if a loudmouth. Yeah, let him in.' He glanced around the casino. There was a game of poker going on at the far end, a couple of his dealers sitting around waiting for business and a Mex shop-owner reading a weeks-old newspaper.

Hagerty opened another bottle of Old Faithful and plonked it before Doc, who took his usual stool at the end of the bar. 'How's your patient?'

'Ah.' Winterhalter sucked in his cheeks considering his first glass, before he tossed it back. 'He's pulling through.'

'Good.' Hagerty gave a throaty laugh. 'I can't wait to run him outa town.'

'Another, Mr Black?' Hagerty returned to his company. 'No doubt you've come to take a look at the maps of your land holdings?'

Black nodded. 'Yeah, we ain't here for long. Hear you've been having a bit of trouble.'

'Yes, my friend Sheriff Cripps started throwing his weight around and paid the price. Damn fool. So we're temporarily without a lawman. But there's nothing I cain't handle.'

'I heard tell you got an unwelcome stranger in your midst.'

'Aw, him? Yeah, a troublemaker. Works for Big Bucks. Been poking his nose in our affairs. But he's out of action right now and, to tell the truth, I think he's gonna stay that way.' He lowered his voice. 'That bumbling drunk quack at the bar don't know his ass from his elbow.'

'I heard that,' Winterhalter called out. He struggled from his stool and walked along to join them, somewhat unsteadily. 'I'll have you know I trained under Dr Heinrich Stritchler, of Heidelberg, the world-reknowned authority on infectious diseases.'

'So what, you soak?' Black spat out. 'Why don't you go back an' join him an' them other lousy Huns. Come on, Hagerty, I wanna take a look at them land holdings over at your office.'

Snipe was in a quandary. He was sure this was the man they were looking for. As Black strode over to the land office he took a bead on him with the Spencer. He was tempted to squeeze the trigger and be done with it. But it would be sheer suicide to take on those eight guards. They looked like professional killers. Of course, if they were here to smoke out the lieutenant that was a different matter. He would give them a fight to remember.

He lowered the carbine and watched Hagerty and Black return from the land office. A short while later both emerged from the casino with the little Mex firecracker, and all three climbed into the coach. Their bodyguards assembled around them and the horses kicked up dust as the coach went wheeling away.

'What's goin' on?' Aaron asked Doc as he returned.

'Beats me. All I heard was small talk,' Winterhalter replied. 'That Mr Black's a very rude gentleman.'

Snipe wondered if he ought to follow the coach, find out what they were up to. 'No,' he muttered to himself, 'the lootenant needs me here.'

Soon after her husband had gone, Jane Hagerty left the casino and hurried across to the surgery. Doc had gone off with his black bag to attend to a labourer who had been hurt in the blasting operations along at her husband's new *haçienda*. She took a look at Slaughter, who was throwing his arms about, his face twitching as he groaned inaudible words. 'We've got to get him out of here,' she insisted. 'Now's our chance.'

Slaughter was drifting in and out of strange dreams, his mind spinning, his insides churning. He heard a woman's voice hissing, 'James, you must wake up. You must try to walk.' She had removed the patch and veil and there were blue eyes beneath a worried brow amid a straggle of fair hair. 'Yeah,' he repeated. 'I must get up.' But he seemed to sink back into a grey mist again.

'Oh, dear, I'm not getting through to him.' Jane walked over to the cabinet, stared at the rows of apothecary's bottles, labels with the names of tinctures she had barely heard of. There was the offending laudanum, the brimstone and other sulphates. 'Doc ought to be ashamed of himself plying him with this stuff.' She noticed another bottle. 'Strychnine! I hope he hasn't been giving him that.'

'If he had the lootenant wouldn't be alive,' Snipe replied, almost jocularly. 'He ain't that tough. That's what they pizen wolves an' coyotes with.'

'Perhaps Doc's not quite right in the head. Come on,' she urged. 'Let's try to hoist him up. We'd better go out the back way. There are too many prying eyes about. I've arranged for Maria's family to take him in.'

Half-dragging, half-walking Slaughter, with his arms around their shoulders, they were on their way when he suddenly doubled up in agony and vomited into the weeds. 'That's right,' Jane soothed, 'get it all out.'

If anybody did see them, as they started off again, they must have thought he'd had a dozen shots of rotgut whiskey too many the way he slumped and staggered, his hair hanging over his eyes, muttering to himself.

'Hey,' he slurred, suddenly coming round, one arm hung around Jane's neck. 'Are you some sorta angel? Ain't I s'posed to be down in Hell?'

She could not help laughing with relief as finally they reached Maria's door and they were ushered in. There were no beds, just straw mats on the floor and Slaughter sank back on to one of these. 'I'm looking after you from now on,' Jane murmured to him, removing his greasy bandages, washing his wounds and gently rubbing in a more soothing ointment. 'Can you sit up and take some broth? That's what you need.'

'What he needs is a good slug of whiskey,' Aaron opined. 'It's like mother's milk to him.'

116

'OK, just a drop, if you think so.' Maria had brought a bowl of soup and, with a splash of whiskey administered by Aaron, Jane attempted to hold up Slaughter's head and spoon some into him. He coughed and dribbled but got some down before sinking back into his dreams. 'I hope he's not going to be too much trouble to you, Maria.'

'You are the one who will be in trouble, Meesis Hagerty,' Maria replied, 'unless you go off home.'

'No need to worry,' Jane replied. 'My husband said he'll be away on business for a few days.'

'I wanna stay here,' Snipe said. 'Is that OK?'

'*Sí*, we got plenty mats,' Maria laughed, 'but not much room.' Indeed, there were three children, her husband and his ancient mother crowded into the small house. Food was cooked on a charcoal burner in a small annexe at the back. A dog and a few chickens which wandered in and out completed the family.

'I got a feelin' I'm gonna enjoy it here.' Aaron had purloined a bottle of Doc's bourbon. He took a swig and passed it to Jorge, Maria's husband. 'Down the hatch, *amigo*. The lootenant told me only to drink good liquor. He don't know what he's missing.'

TEN

East of San Lorenzo flatlands stretched for a hundred miles watered by streams flowing down from the border mountains where the Apache reigned. It was dangerous country but considered fine for grazing cattle and settlers moving into Arizona territory were grabbing what land there was. It was many a man's dream to own their own spread.

Finn Goldsby, and his partner Johnnie Nance, had claimed rights to a ten-mile stretch of good grazing land, built themselves a cabin, and were busy stocking it with longhorns that had run wild and proliferated during the Civil War.

'This is new country, great country,' Finn had told the crafty land agent, Joe Hagerty, when he made him a derisory offer for the spread. 'This is going to be the most prosperous cattle country in

118

the territory, so I ain't selling, no way, no how.'

'We'll see.' Hagerty had given him a mocking grin, mounted his horse and ridden back to town.

But that was several weeks before when Hagerty had had Sheriff Cripps and a bunch of lowdown gunslingers on his payroll. Finn and Johnnie were glad to hear that Cripps and most of his henchmen had been wiped out in a raid on the Rawlings' place. 'Hagerty's on his own now, the last rat in his hole,' Finn told Johnnie.' He couldn't give us no trouble even if he wanted to.'

How wrong could a man be?

'We ain't gonna be Mex'cuns tonight, boys,' the sharp faced Black told his dozen desperadoes as they checked their guns and horses at the hideout. 'We're gonna be Apaches.'

A smile spread across his hard features as he tossed them loin-cloths, headbands, and scalp-hung spears. Such mementoes were easy enough to buy in the townships where they fetched a good price as souvenirs. He opened a tub of theatrical red make-up, like actors use, and dumped it on the ground. 'Here y'are, strip off and daub them lily-white bodies of yourn.'

'What?' one of the hardcases, Jeb Dooley, protested. 'I ain't stripping naked, not fer you, not fer nobody.'

'Ye'll do what ye're told, or clear out.' Black

119

pulled back his coat and fingered the diamond-encrusted revolver on his his belt. 'Come on, you blushing li'l flowers; I'm gonna be the same. Do you wanna earn your cash or not?'

He casually removed his city garments, passing them to his Mexican whore, who shrilled laughter as he stood naked as nature intended. 'What's the matter with *you*?' he asked, menacingly, and she fell silent.

Black hardly needed any paint for he swam most days in the clear pool amid the rocks of their hideout and was tall and tanned. In fact, once he had wound the cloth around his middle, and a scarlet scarf around his head to cover his baldness, he might well have been mistaken for one of that brave and cruel tribe.

'All right,' he shouted, as the men groaned and moaned as they began to undress. 'You can keep your damn boots on. By rights we oughta ride bareback, but I doubt if there'll be many witnesses. Leave your revolvers behind. We just carry carbines, the way they do.'

Dooley, somewhat overweight, managed a comic impression of a redskin and even stuck a feather in his hair. When he was ready, he asked, 'How many of 'em are there?'

'There's Finn Goldsby and Johnnie Nance, Goldsby's wife, and two brats aged about nine and ten. They got four hands but I guess a couple of 'em might be out tending herd.'

'Do we kill 'em all?' Dooley asked. 'I ain't into killin' wimmin and kids. It ain't right.'

Most of the men muttered their agreement. 'Makes me feel dirty, the thought of it,' Dooley said. 'We'll be vilified wherever we go.'

'Aw, Jesus, what a bunch of Sunday-school preachers I got on my hands.' Black daubed a bit of warpaint on his face and chest to show them how. 'All right, you dummies, we'll leave the woman and kids. Maybe we'll just give her a seein' to 'fore we go.'

'You dare,' the Mexican girl spat out, 'I don' spik to you no more.'

Black grabbed her roughly by her hair and kissed her on the lips, then picked up his carbine and leapt on his horse. 'Come on, you milksops. The moon's fit to rise. Let's ride.'

They rode like the wind down from their mountain hideout, galloping across the plain, straight as an arrow for the Goldsby ranch, charging in, screaming and whooping like savages, hurling their burning torches at the cabin roof. There was to be terror under the moon that night.

Johnnie Nance ran out, a shotgun in his hands. He was sent spinning, a bullet from Jeb Dooley in his abdomen, and left lifeless in the dust.

The leader of the 'Apaches', Black, saw Finn

Goldsby standing outside the cabin door, a rifle aimed at the raiders. Black hurled his spear, hitting him in the chest. Goldsby lay kicking and writhing like a landed fish.

His barrel-shaped wife ran from the burning house, dragging her two children, a boy and girl. She screamed at the sight of her husband and ran like a headless chicken amid the mustangs' legs.

Two cowboys clambered out of the low, sod-built bunkhouse, firing six-guns and were soon silenced. Black had pulled out his carbine and rode back and forth looking for any other threat.

They found the terrified woman hiding in the chicken house, shielding her children. Her eyes bulged and she was shivering and shaking like a jelly. Her obvious expectation was to be raped and scalped. But the sound of gunshots distracted the half-naked 'Apaches'. They turned and rode to meet two other cowhands who had been out with the small herd and had raced to help when they heard the shooting, saw the house in flames. They received the same treatment as their comrades from the flashing firearms of a dozen men.

'What about the woman?' Dooley shouted. 'You said—'

'What, that bag of bouncy balloons?' Black turned to him, scornfully. 'She's too fat for me. Come on, we've done enough. Let's git outa here.'

'Is he diseased, or is he bewitched?' Jorge's mother squawked as she squatted beside the sweat-streaming Slaughter laid out on his mat. 'If it's his enemy's done this I can put a spell on him.'

The gnarled old woman, a faded black serape wound tight about her, added in Spanish, 'If it's his stomach that's bad I have the very thing.' She sprinkled the dust of a ground rattlesnake's head into his broth. 'That will cure him.'

Jane looked askance as Mama went off to pick herbs and leaves to make an evil-smelling poultice for his wounds. 'I fear she's going to be more trouble for you than Doc,' she said to Slaughter. 'Here, you must drink lots of water.'

'Water?' Slaughter grimaced as he looked at the gourd and mug she placed by his side. 'Ugh! Never touch it. I don't wanna catch typhus, if I ain't already got it.'

'This is fresh from a mountain spring,' Maria chided him. 'Jorge goes each day to fill bottles to sell in the market place.'

'OK,' Slaughter muttered, wearily, taking a swig. 'I'll try.'

Whether it was the water, or the rattler's head, or the furlough from Doc's treatment, strangely enough, in a day or two the former lieutenant began to feel a lot better and returned to his senses.

'Hey, Aaron, gimme a hand. I gotta git back on

my legs or I'll lose the use of 'em.'

Snipe and Jorge escorted him along to a *cantina* in the main square, and sat in the shade out of the blazing sun. 'Jeez,' Slaughter sighed as he sipped at a milky coffee, 'this is like the best cawfee I ever tasted. I feel as weak as a kitten, but like I'm coming back to life.'

The peaceful scene was suddenly shattered.

'Apaches!' a woman was screaming as she drove a one-horse wagon into San Lorenzo. 'They tried to kill us all.'

People ran to help the barrel-shaped Mrs Goldsby and her two children from the wagon. Her husband, Finn, was laid out in the back. 'He got an Apache spear in him,' she wailed. 'I ain't sure he's gonna live. They kilt everyone else.'

Finn Goldsby was carried over to the *cantina* and his wound examined. 'Doc's outa town,' the blacksmith said.

'Lucky for Finn,' Slaughter muttered. 'You wanna git Jorge's Ma to put a poultice on that.'

Mrs Goldsby was jabbering on about how the red devils were intent on raping and scalping her but she fought them off. 'I was so ferocious, like a mountain lion defending her cubs, in the end they let me be.'

'Where the hell's the army?' a storekeeper asked. 'They're s'posed to be protecting us.'

Just then the Tucson stage came creaking in, its

six horses hauled to a halt in front of the hotel. Joe Hagerty stepped out. By now an angry crowd had gathered and hurried over to shout out at Hagerty as he reached the doorway of his casino. 'What are you going to do about this latest attack, Mr Mayor?' the blacksmith bellowed. 'Or are you too busy making money?'

Hagerty had a bulging carpet-bag in one hand, packed with $10,000, had they but known it. He turned to them and scowled. 'Money is what keeps this town alive. If it weren't for my efforts there'd be no San Lorenzo, no prosperity for you people.'

'Prosperity?' the blacksmith shouted. 'Everybody getting attacked and killed and run off their land so you can buy it up. You call that prosperity?'

'He's a murderer.' Nathan Rawlings' voice rang out from the back of the crowd. 'He may not have pulled the trigger himself, but he killed my pa and brother. I say we hang him.'

'Hold on a minute.' The Revd Ayling had arrived and raised his arms to protest. 'Let's not go to extremes. Let's not blame Joe Hagerty for this latest outrage. He knew nothing about it. He's been away in Tucson on business.'

'Yeah,' Hagerty growled, 'and I got witnesses to prove it. If you wanna know, I been lookin' to the future of this town. I been having talks with the rail company about getting the line running again so your businesses prosper; you farmers can send your fruit and corn to Tucson, and the ranchers can ship their cattle to the beef-hungry markets in California. That's what I've been talking about.'

'He's a lying, swindling murderer.' Nathan had ridden into town on his mule and had his rifle in his hand. 'If you won't hang him, I'll damn well put him down.'

The youth forced his way through the crowd so he could get a bead on Hagerty, who threw wide his arms and shouted, 'I'm unarmed. You know that.'

'Yeah, because you're too yeller to fight,' Nathan cried. 'But I don't care. Mad dogs need putting down.'

He fired the single shot rifle at Hagerty, but the blacksmith knocked the barrel into the air and the lead splintered the woodwork of the casino.

'That ain't no good, Nathan,' the blacksmith hollered, disarming him. 'You go on like that it's you who'll be gittin' hanged – by the law enforcers.'

'We ain't got none,' a woman cried. 'String up Hagerty, I say.'

There was the jingle of harness and clatter of sabres as General Crook and his platoon of weary troops came jogging into the square. 'What's this?' Crook demanded, seeing a man with a hanging noose ready in his hands. 'Not another lynch party, I hope. Fortescue, disperse these people. Send them back to their homes.'

It seemed the general had got news of the so-called Apache attack and had come to investigate. 'In my opinion Cochise is many miles to the west of here,' he said, as he slid from his mule, removed his gauntlets and solar topee. 'We had a fifty-mile ride. We'll camp here tonight. I wish to talk to the survivors.'

When Doc Winterhalter got back from visiting the labourer at the *hacienda* he went to take a look at Finn Goldsby and seemed surprised to see Slaughter lounging there. 'You outa bed?' he asked. 'I been wondering where you got to.'

'Yeah, no thanks to you,' Slaughter said. 'I'm on my feet again.'

'That's the gratitude I get,' Doc sighed. 'For all I do for them.'

'Don't expect to git paid for it,' Slaughter added.

Now the furore had died down, Hagerty, after depositing his cash in his safe, strolled across to see what was going on. 'I offered you a good price for your land, Goldsby,' he said to the dying man. 'Five hundred dollars; it still stands.'

'That's daylight robbery,' Mrs Goldsby protested.

'Take it,' Finn croaked out. 'It ain't no use to us now.'

'You heard him,' Hagerty drawled. 'How you want it, gold coin or cash? You come across to the saloon, Mrs Goldsby, and I'll pay you out.'

Hagerty could not suppress a faint smile

twitching on his lips as he walked back to the casino. The Goldsbys were not to know that he had already been paid $5,000 for that ten-mile stretch by the South California Railroad.

ELEVEN

'Ain't never heard of Apaches wearing spurs.' Slaughter held up a silver rowel he found in the dust near the Goldsbys' burnt-out cabin. 'Nor riding iron-shod mounts, not unless they stole 'em. And it seems funny to me they let the woman live, nor took them kids back to their tribe.'

'Exactly my sentiments,' General Crook agreed, as they took a look around while a detail of his troopers buried the bodies. They had had to fire guns to set off a flock of black vultures who were feasting on the remains when they arrived. 'But if they weren't Apaches what can be the point of these attacks?'

Slaughter was feeling less than fifty per cent his usual self, but the wounds seemed to be healed, and a breakfast of a pound of rare steak had done him the world of good. So he had managed to sling a leg over his mustang and followed along when the 3rd

Cavalry platoon set off on the trail.

'Can I have a look at your map, General?' he asked.

'For what it's worth,' Crook said, spreading it out on his mule's back. 'This whole area needs to be properly surveyed.'

'Waal, I heard a rumour that a prospector called Ed Schieffelin has been nosing around the south-east corner of the territory and it's believed he may well have struck a rich seam of silver.'

'But that's wild Apache country.'

'That's what they told him, that all he'd find would be his own tombstone. If he has struck lucky, it seems like he wants to keep it to himself as long as he can. He don't want to start a stampede. Or maybe he's made some sorta deal with the railroad people.'

'What are you getting at, Lieutenant?'

'Look.' Slaughter traced his finger along the bottom of the map. 'All those properties that have been attacked, and others that have been bought up by Hagerty, lie along this line. Wouldn't that be on a direct line from Tucson, through San Lorenzo, and on to the eastern corner of the territory, the line the railroad would be likely to take, give or take detours around a few hills?'

'By God, I think you've got it, Slaughter!' the general exclaimed. 'If people learn that the railroad's pushing on through here they'll expect to be paid thousands for their options.'

'Yeah, not the measly amounts Hagerty's offering. You well know, Gen'ral, how generous the US Government is with grants for railroads. Hagerty stands to make a fortune from this.'

'Quite,' Crook mused. 'Even if it's not a silver mine the railroad's aiming at, Hagerty, himself, says that this area could become a big cattle centre.'

'With him as the cattle baron?'

The general smiled. 'You don't like him, do you?'

'In my opinion you shoulda arrested him and searched his safe for that stolen money, Gen'ral.'

'I'm afraid we just haven't got the evidence. Nor have I the right in law to do that. I have to accept his claim that he has been acting legitimately as a land agent and knew nothing of the impending attacks on property. So, I fear, my hands are tied.'

'Yeah, I guess the fact that he refuses to carry a gun or fight lets him off the hook.'

'Well, the sooner we catch up with those responsible for the slaughter here,' Crook remarked, 'the sooner we might get some answers.'

'Mind if I tag along, suh?'

'If you can keep up the pace. That's a nasty wound you took.'

'Aw, I'll be OK.'

'Right,' the general exclaimed. 'Fortescue, order the men to mount up. We've another hard ride ahead. I hope my Apache scouts have better luck picking up the trail this time.'

'Yeah, me, too,' Slaughter muttered. 'But I got a feeling we're getting warm.'

Earlier, Slaughter had told Snipe to ride north to Mesquite. 'Ask around, see if Black and Hagerty were seen talking to anybody up there. Anybody suspicious, that is. Try to follow Black's trail.'

'Hell's bells, James,' Aaron exclaimed. 'You must still be feeling groggy. That trail's a week old and gone cold by now.'

'Just do it,' Slaughter had snapped.

So when he reached Mesquite Aaron called in on Maggie McLeuclar knowing that passengers on the weekly stage from Tucson would take refreshments at her eating-house while the horses were changed at the livery across the road. Perhaps Black and Hagerty had done the same.

'Yes, it's no secret,' she cried. 'Didn't them two gobble down a plateful of my scones and sup my coffee in this very house which ye made such a sorry sight?'

'Yep, but how's about after they'd had their scones?'

'I'm not one to be tittle-tattling about my clients, but yon land agent Hagerty went over the road and hired a horse and buggy to set off on the Tucson trail.'

'What about the stagecoach and outriders?'

'I've no time to be spying on strangers, but it did seem to head off the trail up over there.'

'Which direction did they go?'

'To the north-east. I recall thinking it very strange for there's nothing to be found in those mountains. Ye'll as soon find a man on the moon.'

After resting his mustang a few hours and enjoying a plate of the Scots' lady's pork pies, Aaron pressed on. Yes, there were coach tracks and horses' prints, sure enough. But where were they going? The country was, indeed, like a lunar landscape. Great boulders were scattered as if by some giant's hand, wind-eroded rocks took strange forms, and at ground level there was sage brush, mesquite, cactus and spiky Spanish bayonet. The terrain gradually rose to about 3,000 feet and, as Snipe followed the buggy tracks weaving through the obstacles, he noted that they appeared to be aimed towards a high rim of a deep basin.

Suddenly the tracks ceased and Aaron scratched the back of his head with bewilderment until he saw that one of the huge rocks was not rock but a grey tarpaulin hanging over a large conveyance.

'Gor swizzle!' he exclaimed as he jerked the tarpaulin away to reveal Black's stage coach. 'That slope's too steep for 'em. They musta climbed up there with the hosses.'

What, he wondered, would he find on the other side of the rim?

133

The two Apache scouts, stunted men with Mongolian cast of features, ran on in front of General Crook's troopers. As before after five miles or so the raiders had broken apart, scattering to throw off any pursuers. But the general was confident they were heading in a north-westerly direction and pressed on. He was rewarded by seeing one of the Apaches beckoning excitedly as he found deep hoofprints and picked up the trail again.

'Such marvellous stamina these scouts have,' Crook remarked. 'Do you notice how they have developed huge chests and terrific thigh muscles in their short legs from all the running and leaping from rock to rock?'

The hale and hearty Crook hardly ever showed any sign of exhaustion but, as he sat his mule and turned to Slaughter, he saw him grimace and clutch at his chest wound, swaying in the saddle. 'Good Lord, man!' he cried. 'You're in no condition for this. You should be taking it easy with that wound for at least another couple of weeks.'

Slaughter muttered through gritted teeth, 'I'm OK.'

'You are certainly not. You are going back to San Lorenzo immediately, Lieutenant. That's an order.'

'I ain't in your army, Gen'ral. You cain't give me orders.'

'Come on, man, don't be a fool,' the general coaxed more gently. 'Be a sensible chap. Off you go. Oh, just a minute.' He took a pad from his pocket and scribbled on it. 'Give this to the sergeant of my baggage train. I hope to meet up with him in Mesquite if we continue across country. God only knows when.'

Sweat was pouring from Slaughter, his head spinning, so he took the note and nodded. 'Good hunting, Gen'ral. I'd like to have been in at the kill. I'll keep an eye on Hagerty, instead.'

The troopers rode for miles across country, unmapped and unexplored, a maze of forbidding brakes and deep canyons. Grook urged them on, following a clear stream lined with wild hops, a heady perfume. 'This must be what the 'Pache make their beer from,' he remarked to Fortescue, as if they were out for a nature stroll.

His young aide-de-camp was looking more and more dishevelled and strained. 'Hadn't we better rest the mounts, sir? We must have come more than thirty miles.'

'I want to try to reach the ridge of that plateau,' Crook replied, studying it through his telescope. 'We're gradually gaining on it. There seems to be some sort of basin on the other side possibly caused by a volcanic eruption in times past.'

'Yes, sir,' Fortescue responded meekly and gave

the signal to advance.

As they climbed to the crest they left behind vegetation of yucca, mescal, nopal, giant cactus and hediondilla, as the general knowledgeably pointed out, and gained a sprinkle of tree covering, scrub pine, cedar, oak, and the madrono, or mountain mahogany.

They gained the heights after a hard ascent and General Crook instructed his troop to ground hitch their horses as he did his mule. His rifle in hand he led the way, crawling like an Indian to peer over the ridge.

'My God! Just look at that,' he hissed to Fortescue. 'Have you ever seen the like?'

Montezuma's Well, as it had been named by the few frontiersmen who had ever penetrated so far into this mountain range dropped from the ridge into a semi-circle of steep red cliffs into which had been hewn prehistoric dwellings, some six storeys high. In its centre was a lakelet of torquoise water some eighty feet in depth. It was in this Black enjoyed his morning bathe for he had established the Well as his HQ.

'There they are, boys,' Crook called in a low voice, for below them they could see a dozen or so men, some sitting by the Well where a cooking fire smoked, others strolling in and out of the caves and buildings as if they hadn't a care in the world. 'But how are we going to get at 'em?'

'We could make our way down along *there*, sir,' Fortescue said, pointing. 'There seems to be some sort of precipitous path.'

'Yes, perhaps.' Crook had his 'scope to his eye again. 'The trouble is they would immediately spot us and be off on their horses again.'

The two scouts were behaving in an agitated manner. 'This place no good,' one grimaced. 'Haunted. Bad spirits. We no go down.'

'Really? No doubt that's why the Apache give it a wide berth. Aha, who's this? A gentleman in a frock coat. If I'm not mistaken that would be our Mr Black. Good Lord! He's only wearing one spur. That must be him.'

'What are you going to do, sir?'

'I've decided to dispense arbitrary justice. Not my usual practice, I know.' Crook tucked his 'scope away, and rested his rifle on a rock, getting Black in his sights. 'I'm positive he's our man. He gave little mercy to those train travellers and settlers, did he?'

'Shall I give the command to fire, sir.'

'Yes.' Crook squinted one-eyed. 'After my shot.'

The report of the rifle barrelled away, its echo bouncing off the cliffs. At that moment Black had kneeled down to the fire. The bullet took of his hat, sending it spinning. 'Damn. Missed!'

All eyes below were upturned with apprehension as a fusillade of gunfire poured down upon them from the ridge. Some scattered to find their carbines, others pulled revolvers and tried to hide behind rocks. Most were trapped around the pool. They quickly returned fire but could find no targets apart from puffs of smoke and flashes from rifle barrels. The troopers were well concealed. The first outlaw to be hit back-pedalled into the pool. Others were soon being swatted like flies.

'Who the hell is it?' Black cried, as he tried to conceal himself behind a rock. He had already emptied his revolver at those on the rim to no effect. He looked around and saw another of his men clutch at his abdomen and collapse as blood flowered on his shirt. 'I'm outa lead. Keep fightin', boys. Cover me while I go git a box of ammo.'

He grabbed up his hat as he went dodging away through the rocks and bent double made for the cave where they kept their stores. But, as he passed the corral, he changed his mind.

'We ain't got a chance,' he muttered, and swung open the gate. His own black stallion was already saddled, a carbine in the boot. He glanced back furtively to see if he had been watched, but the remains of his men were too busy blamming away with their guns as the battle raged to notice what he was up to. He quickly herded the four grey coach horses out of the corral and jumped into the saddle. 'Hyargh!' he yelled, 'Git!'

The Mexican girl came sprinting from their cave swinging his pair of leather saddle-bags in her hand.

'I got your money,' she yelled.

'Thanks.' He reached down to grab it from her as a bullet whistled past his head.

'Take me weeth you,' she pleaded, offering her hand.

Black kicked her back into the dust. 'Get lost, sweetheart.'

He spun the stallion away and set off at a gallop after the coach horses, heading towards Mesquite. He kept his head well down until he was out of range and looking back gave a scoffing grin. 'Well, at least I didn't have to pay the boys.'

A cloud of dust kicked up as Black charged down from the rim of the basin, alerted Aaron, who at first thought it must be half-a-dozen riders or more. He was at the point of negotiating along a goat path above a *barranca* whose steep side dropped at least 500 feet. 'I can take 'em,' he gritted out, raising his Ben Henry. He had fifteen metal-cased .44 calibre bullets in the magazine. He cocked the hammer and tried to aim from horseback at the leading rider who appeared out of the haze, half-a-mile away. But his mustang suddenly stumbled, lost its footing and, to his horror, Aaron encountered vast space opening out in front of him. The horse tumbled forwards and, not having the reins in his hands, Aaron was pitched from the saddle.

He landed with a thud on the cliff face some thirty feet down and watched the horse go spinning to its death on the rocks below. Scratched and shaken, Aaron had the sickening sensation that his leg was broken. He lay there waiting for Black to arrive and administer the kiss of death.

But Black had not seen him and went riding past on the path above, the four stage mares naturally following the leading stallion. 'Jeez!' Aaron gave a whistle. 'That was a close one.'

But, as he lay there, he suddenly realized that his right leg was useless. He was never going to be able to climb out of there. Up in the blue sky vultures were already circling, waiting for him to die. 'Hot damn,' he groaned. 'I've lost me rifle, too.'

When he returned to San Lorenzo Slaughter bumped into Nathan. 'Did you sell your land to Joe Hagerty?' he asked.

'No, I'd rather sell it to the devil.' The wiry young man brushed his fair hair from his eyes. 'I wish I'd killed him when I had the chance.'

'Yeah, well, you better watch out he don't have the same idea about you. Many a man's met his end from a surprise shot in the dark.'

'Well, the same applies to you, Mr Slaughter, don't it?'

'Guess I'm top of Hagerty's list.' The former bounty hunter brandished his Spencer as he dismounted. 'I keep this close at hand. You oughta think about gettin' yourself better protection than that squirrel gun.'

Nathan shrugged. 'Pa's money's all but gone after the funeral expenses. I've moved with Ma into Widow Lovel's boarding-house. I've sold off the livestock at the farm, but I've gotta get myself some sort of work 'fore I can think of tryin' to rebuild the cabin agin.'

'I'd help y'out if I could,' Slaughter said, 'but I'm down to my last few dollars myself. I'm back to sleepin' in the straw alongside my hoss.'

That was where Jane Hagerty found him later that morning, in a stall at the livery, laid out on a bed of hay. 'I guess I overdid it,' he said. 'The gen'ral sent me back. How's Joe?'

Jane had a serape wrapped around her and over her head, possibly for purposes of disguise, for she had been forbidden to contact Slaughter again. 'Things are somewhat strained.' She made a grimace of her lips. 'Why did you leave Maria's?'

'Aw, I've been enough of a burden to her. And to tell the truth I'd had my fill of the ministrations of that old witch of a mother of her'n. No doubt she meant well.'

Jane produced a small pair of surgical scissors. 'Let's have a a look at your wound.' She touched the skin of his ribcage gently with her fingers. 'Yes, I think it's time to take out the stitches. Hold still.'

When she had done unsnipping them she smiled. 'You'll have a nice scar.'

'It won't be the first.' As she leaned over him he caught hold of her and kissed her lips. Jane tensed, but for moments relaxed and responded. 'I been wanting to do that for a long time,' he breathed out, as she broke away.

'James, please, I don't think this is a good idea.' She was wearing a brightly-coloured Mexican skirt and loose peasant blouse beneath the shawl. As they lay together on the straw Slaughter's horny hand slid beneath the material to fondle her breasts. 'No, really!'

She pulled apart and sat up as he caught hold of her hand. He groaned, 'Somethang tells me I'm kinda fully recovered, thanks to you, darlin'.'

'Yes, I gathered that.' Jane gazed at him, sadly. 'It's no good. I know he's a bully, a coward, possibly a murderer, but I'm married to him. I made my wedding vows, James. I've got to stick by them until such time as I get a divorce. I hate deceit. I can't go into some hole-in-the-corner affair with you.'

'Maybe you don't fancy sleeping in a barn with some down-and-out drifter,' he said. 'I cain't blame you. What the hell sorta life can I offer you? Although, I gotta say you're the first woman in a long time I've felt like throwing a rope over.'

'Is that a peculiar proposal of marriage?'

'I guess so.'

'Did you really kill her . . . your wife?'

He peered up at her through his long strands of

black hair. 'Yep. A moment of madness I've regretted every day since.'

'What happened?'

'We were childhood sweethearts. I was away fightin' in the war for four years. When I got home I found her in bed with some Yankee officer.'

'Poor girl. She must have been so lonesome.'

'Yeah, I guess she was. That didn't occur to me at the time.'

Jane sighed and studied him. 'Can't you settle down, start anew? Forget all that?'

'I guess I could. I'm kinda tired of killing. I fancy buying a li'l spread, raising horses.'

She finally pulled her hand away. 'I don't want to be an adulteress, Lieutenant. I always think, if a woman does that to one man, how could her second husband trust her?'

'That's a point.' Slaughter grinned and felt at his crotch. 'Guess I'll just have to go visit the bath house again.'

She looked at him sharply. 'What do you mean?'

'Waal, there's a li'l Mex gal who's got a real nice touch when she's groping around for the soap.'

Jane Hagerty fell silent for a bit as she knelt beside him. 'I don't think I like the sound of that.'

'Well, if you're bidding me an eternal *adieu*, what else am I s'posed to do? I guess you still have relations with your husband?'

The young woman visibly shuddered. 'I can't

143

bear him touching me.'

'But you let him? So—'

She stood up, hurriedly. 'I had better go. Take care, James. I'll pray for you.'

He leaned on one elbow and watched her lithe figure as she left the barn. 'That's nice to know,' he called after her, somewhat bitterly.

TWELVE

Jagged daggers of forked lightning flashed across the night sky, lighting up the houses of San Lorenzo like some stage setting a million times intensified. Thunder rumbled over Boboquivari and the other mountain ranges as dense black clouds rolled towards the desert town.

Through this wild night came galloping four grey horses pulling a light stagecoach with a fiery stallion hitched to the back. Black, on the box, hauled it in front of the casino and jumped down. It had gone one in the morning and most folk were cowering in their beds trying to close their ears to the sound of the storm. Black hurried inside. Joe Hagerty, smartly attired as always, was standing behind the bar talking to Doc Winterhalter who was on his customary corner stool drinking a whiskey.

'Tell 'em you're closed,' Black snapped, glancing at a group of men around the blackjack table.

145

'There's been trouble.'

Hagerty went over to usher the men out and when he returned asked, 'What's wrong?'

'I've brought the rest of the cash from the train robbery.' Black opened his saddle-bags and tipped out the bundles of notes. 'There's seven thousand. I ain't had to pay anybody out. They're probably all dead by now. The army ambushed us at the hideout. I was lucky to escape.'

'Get the rest from your safe, Joe,' Winterhalter ordered. 'And what you've been paid by the railroad boys for the land. I've a pretty good idea how much. So don't try to cheat us.'

'You know me,' Hagerty replied. 'I wouldn't do that. I'm happy with my third share.'

'I'll come with you.' Black pulled aside his frock coat to reveal the $500-diamond-studded revolver in his belt. 'Just make sure you don't hide none.'

The ruddy-faced Doc was drumming his fingers on the bar as if in a hurry to be done when they emerged from the back office. 'You sure you ain't left none over at the land office, Joe?'

'No, it ain't safe over there. I bring everything over here at night. What is this? Don't you trust me?'

'Sure we do.' Doc smiled amiably, tossed back his drink and said, 'Let's go over to the table in the corner outa the way and divvy up, shall we? The Three Musketeers, that's us. One for all and all for

146

one. Or perhaps you haven't read that romance?'

'Fair shares,' Black agreed, sitting down and splitting all the cash into three piles. 'Seven thousand three hundred dollars each, more or less. You can have the odd seventy-five, Joe, for playing your part so well. You an' Doc certainly had this town fooled.'

'Well, Doc did.' Hagerty grinned as he tucked his wads of greenbacks away into a carpet-bag. 'He almost fooled me at times. I guess it's time for me to head for California.'

'What, with your lovely young wife?' Black raised a crafty eyebrow to wink at Winterhalter who was standing behind Hagerty's chair. 'Where is she?'

'Upstairs asleep. She—' Joe Hagerty gave a strangled gasp and flailed his arms as Doc's scalpel slit his jugular. He fell to the floor, blood spouting all over his fine suit.

The two men watched him as his hard, handsome face took on the fixed and rapt expression of death. 'So long, Joe,' Winterhalter said, as he put his scalpel back in its velvet-lined case and slid it into his pocket. 'Pleasant dreams.'

Thunder suddenly crashed out like a giant orchestra of drums and cymbals overhead, and vivid lightning sliced the night illuminating the conspirators in mockery of the puny eleven flickering candles. 'So that's eleven thousand each now,' Doc shouted above it. 'I believe it's time we departed this town. The game, as they say, is done.'

'Yeah, let's get out! Mexico here we come. Not much of a night for travelling. But you can go inside the coach. You'll be all right. You always are, aincha, Doc?'

'I get by,' Winterhalter agreed, 'and with me doing the planning you don't do so badly. This calls for a celebratory drink before we're off.' He finished packing his share of the cash into his doctor's black bag and went behind the bar to find a bottle of best bourbon. 'I'll take a coupla bottles with us. I'm not fond of Mexican firewater.'

'I'll be right with you.' Black dumped his packed saddle-bags on the table. 'I'll go get that feisty blonde wife of his. I really fancy her. She's coming with us. And when I've done with her she'll fetch a pretty price south of the border.'

'Excellent idea.' Winterhalter brought a horn-handled hunting knife from his pocket. 'This belongs to that boy Nathan. I slipped it out of his sheath in the crowd.' He stuck it hard into Hagerty's throat and left it embedded. 'He had good cause to hate our friend. Now he'll be the one they hang.'

'You think of everything, chief.' Black grinned and headed for the stairs. 'Now, where is that young lady? At least, with all this racket going on nobody will hear her screams.'

*

148

Slaughter was standing at the door of the livery anxiously watching the lightning display when Nathan Rawlings came running towards him.

'What's wrong?' he shouted.

'There's that coach come into town. I saw it pass my window. It hauled up outside the casino. There's somethang funny going on, Mr Slaughter.'

Suddenly the threatening clouds opened up and rain rattled down in hailstones turning the dust to muddy puddles in no time. 'Come on,' Slaughter yelled. 'Here, take my Schofield.'

The heavens crashed out again like gods having a mighty battle up above as they ran towards the main square. Black came from the casino dragging Jane Hagerty with him. He had manacled her wrists before her with a lawman's handcuffs. Her nightdress and hair were flapping wildly in the storm and she screamed as a streak of lightning hit the roof of the casino, illuminating the night around them, and the dry timbers burst into flames. Black hurled her down the steps and threw her into the coach as the horses reared and plunged with fear. He unlocked one of the manacles and attached her securely to the open window frame.

'Get in with her,' he shouted at Doc, and clambered up on to the box to take the reins.

Jane was kicking and hitting out with her free hand, managing to punch the medic in the nose.

'You bitch.' Winterhalter pulled a two-shot .28

149

calibre Hopkins and Allen pistol from his boot and cracked her across the jaw, then made the mistake of going round to the far side of the coach to climb in the other side.

'Hold it, Doc,' Slaughter shouted. 'Don't make a move.'

Winterhalter turned to him, a snarl on his face, and fired the .28 at the rain-sodden man. Slaughter's Spencer cracked out and the heavy slug twisted in the German's heart sending him flying back to hit the coach wheel.

'Hargh!' Black shouted, and released the brake to send the horses starting away.

Slaughter ran forward, levering another bullet into the breech and aiming at Black as a blob of lightning exploded in his eyes, scorching the Spencer to send it spinning from his hands, the shock knocking him into the mud.

Nathan was luckier, he ran and leaped on to the back of the coach and as it went careering away at a gallop on the trail out of town towards the frontier, he hauled himself on to the top. He pulled the Schofield from his belt and fumbled to thumb the hammer as Black turned, standing in the driver's seat to aim his long-barrelled revolver at the youth's chest point blank. But the coach hit a rock and gave a lurch. Black's bullet seared Nathan's temple. The youth squeezed the Schofield's trigger and made no mistake. Black gasped out with pain and fury and

150

was sent flying from the box like a black-clothed bat.

The reins had gone adrift and the coach was in danger of imminent overturn as Nathan leaped for the back of one of the rear greys and, although it was streaming wet and slippery hung on, working his way forward to the lead horse. He used all his strength to bring the coach to a halt. He soothed the horses, slid to the ground and went to see to the passenger.

'Are you all right, Mrs Hagerty?' he asked.

'I guess so,' she said, stroking her bruised jaw. 'Where is he?'

'Who? Black? He's back on the trail. I believe he's dead. I'll go see if I can find the key to these manacles in his pocket. Then I'll drive the team back.'

The storm was passing over. The sky was clearing. But the Hotel San Lorenzo was well ablaze. There was no saving it as its crackling timbers crashed.

'Kinda poetic justice,' Slaughter muttered as he stood amid the crowd who had gathered. 'They did that to plenty others.'

When the black stagecoach returned Jane stepped from it and ran to Slaughter as he hugged her into his arms. 'Thank God!' she cried. 'I thought you must be dead.'

'Naw.' He grinned widely as he kissed her forehead. 'It give me a hell of a kick that bolt of lightning. By rights I oughta be a pile of smouldering ashes. But it seems like I'm still here. Ain't I a lucky man?'

'Where's your husband, Mrs Hagerty?' the blacksmith asked, as he organized a bucket chain to try to protect adjoining buildings.

'He's inside. He was already dead before the fire. They slit his throat.'

The flames illuminated their faces and dried their sopping wet clothes as they stood before the hotel and watched its demise. 'I'm glad to see it go,' she whispered, as she hung on to Slaughter's waist.

'Look what I found.' Nathan came over to them on the prancing black stallion brandishing the diamond-studded revolver. 'It was on the side of the trail.'

'Finder's keepers. I figure you get to keep the horse and the gun. To the victor the spoils,' the former lieutenant told him. 'You done well, Nathan.'

'There's a hell of a lot of money in their bags inside the coach.'

'Ah, well, we'll have to sort that out.'

As the fire slowed, and after looking at the bodies of Doc and Black, who were laid on the sidewalk outside the undertaker's, the folks drifted back to their beds.

The storm had ceased and all was calm again.

'You ain't got no bed to go to,' Slaughter said.

'Maybe I should share yours in the livery. That

hay looked very comfortable.' Jane hugged him to her, kissing him. 'I'm a widow lady now, after all.'

'You sure?' He turned around and they headed arm in arm towards the livery. 'Ah, waal, I never argue with a woman.'

THIRTEEN

'It's my opinion that German fraudster planned to maintain his cover as a bumbling drunken medic to the end,' Slaughter opined, as he and Jane rode together towards Mesquite. 'That's why he blamed Joe for all the killings and your husband went along with it not aware that they planned to cut him out, too. Doc sure had me fooled for a bit.'

'That's probably why he tried to slowly poison you rather than just have you shot,' Jane mused. 'It was lucky for you I rumbled him.'

'Sure is, sweetheart. Seems like he started his illustrious career in Boston by poisoning fifty old ladies for their inheritance, lulling 'em with his charmin' bedside manner. That was before he teamed up with Black and hit the West with his murderous schemes.'

Slaughter jogged along the winding trail

through the desolate ravines on his mustang and patted a banker's cheque just received through the post from the Kansas City authorities as the reward on Winterhalter's head. He had been wanted dead or alive. 'There could be more comin' in. Never thought he'd prove a big earner for me.'

Big Bucks had honoured his agreement to pay him a sixth of his stolen cash, so one way or another, Slaughter was in the money. And instead of blowing it all, as was his wont in times past, he had bought into a partnership with Nathan to run horses and cattle on the land left after the railroad had taken its ten mile slice. They were in talks to buy out the widows Goldsby and Warrenburg, too, who had decided to open stores in San Lorenzo. They had had enough of the pioneering life.

On top of this the citizens of San Lorenzo had more or less begged Slaughter to pin on the town sheriff's badge at sixty dollars a month. He didn't anticipate much more trouble so he could combine his duties with working the ranch.

'So, all in all, after bein' blown up, half-pizened, and hit by lightning, it seems like I've ended up in clover, don't it?' he called to her. 'Specially as I got a gal like you 'n'all.'

'You sure have, cowboy,' Jane said with a smile. 'Who'd have thought I'd marry that insolent, filthy prairie rat who tried his luck with me.'

155

Wed they were, however, three days before at the Baptist church at San Lorenzo. Then they had decided to head for Mesquite to find out how Snipe was faring and pay him his share of the bounty.

'You ain't the only one who's married, Lootenant.' Aaron was laid out on a cot, his leg in splints. 'I've tied the knot myself.'

'Yeah?' Slaughter was surely surprised. 'Who to?'

'Whoja think?' He indicated the former Mrs McLeuclar, who was busy at the stove. 'The lovely Maggie there. I persuaded her.'

'Aye, he's a new man.' Mrs Snipe's granite features creased into a smile. 'Aaron's found the light of God.'

'Yes, it was while I was perched on that cliffside, poised twixt life and death,' Aaron explained. 'Those beady-eyed vultures had gathered, watching and waiting for me to die. For the first time in my life I prayed. There'd been a lot of shooting up on the mountain top and then a long silence. I thought whoever it was must have rode off t'other way. Those vultures started to edge closer to their breakfast. I guess the general must have been sorting things out up there, for suddenly I heard a bugle, a thunder of hoofs, and the troopers came riding down. I fired off the last shot from my pistol. The Lord musta heard my prayer for Crook himself stuck his head over the edge and tossed a rope down to me. He instructed two of his troopers to

156

carry me back here while he went on his way. They did so and Mrs McLeuclar took me in and cared for me.'

'Hot diggity!' Slaughter shouted. 'Sounds like we got a lot to celebrate. I got a bottle of the Revd Bourbon's special brew outside in my saddle-bag. I'll go get—'

'No, sir, Lootenant.' Aaron held up his hand to halt him. 'I've sworn a solemn oath. Not a drop of spiritous likker shall pass 'tween my lips ever again. I'm reborn. I'm a Presbyterian.'

'No more cursing. No more killing. No more idleness. No more chasing after loose women,' Maggie proclaimed. 'I've converted Mr Snipe to my true religion.'

'Who needs likker?' Aaron made a grab and pulled his bony wife to him. 'Not me when I've got you, beautiful!'

'Och, get away with you.' A blush crept over Maggie's gaunt cheeks as she fluttered her eyelashes. 'It's my pork pies is all you're after.'

Slaughter sniffed the succulent aroma drifting from the stove. 'Can you blame him?'

'Ach, they'll be burnt to a cinder.' Mrs Snipe leapt to her feet and grabbed a rag to draw a tray of crisp pork pies from the oven. 'Can we persuade you two newly-weds to stay the night and join us for supper?'

Slaughter gave Jane a squeeze and a kiss on the

cheek. 'That's an offer we cain't refuse.' He smiled as he propped his Spencer against the wall and eased his gunbelt. 'Draw your chair up to the table, darling. I'm starving.'